Garden City: The Legacy

Cece Vance

Copyright © 2025 Author Name

All rights reserved.

ISBN: **9798241226655**

DEDICATION

To my Aunt Jane — your wisdom, your strength, and your love shaped the foundation of who I am. Every lesson you poured into me lives inside these pages. I miss your voice, your guidance, and your gentle spirit, but your legacy walks with me every day. This book is a tribute to everything you taught me about family, faith, and resilience.

To Bobbi Jr — your memory is a light that will never dim. You are forever part of the bloodline, forever part of our story, and forever loved. Your presence is felt in every chapter, every emotion, every moment of truth.

To my children, bonus children, and grandbabies — you are my purpose, my joy, and my greatest blessing. Everything I create, I create with you in mind. Thank you for loving me, supporting me, and believing in my dreams even when they stretched beyond what we could see.

To my husband — your strength, patience, and steady love have carried me through every late night and every creative storm. Thank you for standing beside me through it all.

To my mother, my mother-in-law, my sister-in-law, my brother-in-law, my aunts, and my entire extended family — your encouragement has been a gift. You are the roots that keep me grounded and the wind that keeps me moving forward.

And to every reader who stepped into the 44 with me — thank you for embracing these characters, for feeling their struggles, and for walking this journey from the first page to the last. You are now part of the legacy too. This book is for the ones who came before us, the ones walking beside us, and the ones rising after us.

This is for **the bloodline**. This is for **the legacy**.

CONTENTS

Chapter 1— After the Smoke Clears

Chapter 2 — Aunt Jane's Warning

Chapter 3 — Corey Under Watch

Chapter 4 — Red's Circle Tightens

Chapter 5— The Block Starts Choosing

Chapter 6 — Pastor Campbell's Visit

Chapter 7 — Kayla Steps In

Chapter 8— Natasha's Accusation

Chapter 9— Bev Draws the Line

Chapter 10 — Corey's First Test

Chapter 11 — Bobbi Jr's Shadow

Chapter 12— The Snitch on the Block

Chapter 13 — Red Sends His Warning

Chapter 14 — The Blocks speaks

Chapter 15 — The Block turns cold

Chapter 16 — Red makes his moves

Chapter 17- Tightening the phone

Chapter 18 — The block shifts again

Chapter 19 — The snitch slips up

Chapter 20— Pressure on the snitch

Chapter 21 — Cracks in the snitch

Chapter 22— Desperation on the block

Chapter 23 — The snitch starts to unravel

Chapter 24 — Red's Shadow on the streets

Chapter 25— Inside the house

Chapter 26 — The house holds it breath

Chapter 27 — The target revealed

Chapter 28— Pressure in the walls

Chapter 29- The walls start talking

Chapter 30- The weight of what's coming

Chapter 31- The engine in the dark

Chapter 32- The engine that wouldn't leave

Chapter 33- The bang that split the bloodline

ACKNOWLEDGMENTS

To my family — thank you for standing with me through every chapter of this journey. Your love, your patience, and your belief in me have carried this series from an idea to a legacy. To my children, bonus children, and grandbabies — you are my heartbeat, my inspiration, and the reason I push forward with purpose. To my husband — thank you for your strength, your support, and your steady presence through every late night and early morning.

To my mother, my mother-in-law, my sister-in-law, my brother-in-law, my aunts, and my entire extended family — your encouragement has been a blessing. You have poured into me in ways that shaped not only this book, but the woman behind it.

To Aunt Jane — your wisdom, your love, and your spirit live in every page of this series. I miss your voice, your guidance, and your gentle strength. You taught me to lead with compassion, to stand firm in truth, and to honor the bloodline. This book is a tribute to everything you poured into me.

To Bobbi Jr — your memory is woven into the heart of this story. Your legacy lives on through the characters, the emotion, and the truth behind every scene. You will always be part of the bloodline.

To my readers — thank you for walking with me through the 44. Thank you for embracing these characters, for feeling their struggles, and for rooting for their survival. Your messages, your support, and your excitement have fueled me through every twist and turn. You are the reason this story lives beyond the page.

To the creative spirit within me — thank you for never letting me quit, even when the journey felt heavy. Thank you for reminding me that stories heal, stories teach, and stories connect us to one another.

And finally, to everyone who believes in the power of family, resilience, and legacy — this book is for you.

CHAPTER ONE — AFTER THE SMOKE CLEARS

The sun hadn't even risen yet, but the 44 was already awake, sitting under a heavy silence that felt more like a warning than peace. Dee stood in the doorway of the house, staring at the street where everything went wrong the night before. The chalk outline was gone and the blood had been washed away, but the memory of Red's message still clung to the concrete like it was carved into it. Corey stepped beside him, hoodie up, eyes scanning the block the way Dee taught him, whispering that it was quiet. Dee shook his head and told him it was too quiet. Inside, the house moved slow. Bev's hands trembled as she tried to make coffee. Aunt Jane whispered prayers behind her closed door. Bobbi Jr sat at the table staring into nothing, guilt wrapped around him like a second skin. Chris and Tim circled the house, checking windows, locks, and shadows. The family wasn't just on edge — they were on alert.

Dee finally stepped inside and told everyone to get up because they needed to talk. Bev told him they were tired, but he reminded her that Red wasn't tired and he wasn't done. Aunt Jane stepped out of her room, leaning on the frame, telling them Red was testing them, watching how they moved. Bobbi Jr whispered that Red was coming for him, but Aunt Jane shook her head and said he already had — now he was coming for the ones he loved. Corey asked what they were supposed to do, and Dee looked around the room at everyone he loved before saying they would tighten up, move smart, and move together.

Before anyone could respond, a soft knock hit the door — three taps, familiar but out of place. Bev frowned, wondering who would be there this early. Dee opened the door and found Pastor Campbell standing there with his hat in his hand and concern in his eyes. The pastor stepped inside, saying he heard there was trouble and he came to pray with them because the enemy was moving fast and they needed covering. Dee exhaled, admitting things were getting bad, and Pastor Campbell placed a hand on his shoulder, telling him darkness always gets loudest right before it loses.

Before they could gather, another knock hit the door — this one sharp and impatient. Dee opened it to find Kayla standing there, briefcase in hand, heels clicking on the porch. She walked in without waiting for an invitation and said they needed to talk because Red's people were moving money and someone on the block was talking. Bev's eyes widened at the mention of a snitch, and Kayla confirmed it, saying the person was close.

But before anyone could process that, a voice came from behind Kayla. Natasha stepped forward with her arms crossed and her attitude loud, saying she needed to talk too. She announced she was pregnant, and if Dee didn't handle it with her, she was going to Cece with it. The room erupted — Bev gasped, Corey cursed under his breath, Kayla rolled her eyes, and Aunt Jane closed hers like she needed strength from heaven. Dee stared at Natasha and told her the baby wasn't his, but Natasha only smirked and said they would see.

Pastor Campbell sighed and whispered for the Lord to give him patience. And just like that, the day had barely begun, and the war for the bloodline was already knocking on every door.

CHAPTER TWO — AUNT JANE'S WARNING

The house felt too small once everyone crowded into the living room, the air thick with tension from Natasha's accusation, Kayla's news, and Pastor Campbell's quiet concern. Dee stood in the center of it all, jaw tight, trying to keep the anger from boiling over. Natasha's footsteps were still echoing down the walkway outside, and Bev was pacing back and forth, muttering under her breath about how she knew that girl was trouble from the start. Corey leaned against the wall with his arms crossed, shaking his head, saying this was the last thing they needed with Red circling the block like a shark. Kayla sat on the arm of the couch, flipping through her folder, her voice calm but sharp as she explained that Red's people were moving money in patterns that didn't make sense unless someone close was feeding him information. She said she didn't know who yet, but she would find out, and when she did, the family needed to be ready for what that meant.

Pastor Campbell stood quietly near the window, watching the street like he could feel the spiritual weight sitting on the block. He finally spoke, saying the enemy didn't always come with violence — sometimes he came with confusion, distraction, and division. He told them that the devil loved to slip through cracks in the family, and right now, the cracks were showing. Bev stopped pacing long enough to ask him what they were supposed to do when the streets didn't care about prayer. Pastor Campbell told her prayer wasn't weakness — it was armor — and they needed all the armor they could get.

Aunt Jane's door opened slowly, and the room fell silent as she stepped out, her presence commanding even in her frailty. She looked at each of them, her eyes sharper than her body allowed her to move. She told them that Red wasn't just attacking them physically — he was attacking their unity, their peace, their foundation. She said the enemy always tried to break the family before he broke the body, and right now, he was doing a good job. Dee swallowed hard, asking her what she meant, and Aunt Jane told him that Natasha showing up wasn't an accident, the snitch on the block wasn't a coincidence, and the fear sitting in the house wasn't random. She said Red was pushing them into chaos so they would make mistakes.

Bobbi Jr finally spoke, his voice low and heavy, saying he felt like all of this was his fault. Aunt Jane shook her head and told him guilt was a trap, and if he let it take root, it would destroy him faster than Red ever could. She told him he needed to stand up, face what he'd done, and protect the family instead of hiding behind shame. Corey stepped closer to him, placing a hand on his shoulder, telling him they were in this together whether he liked it or not.

Kayla closed her folder and said she needed to start digging immediately, but she needed access to certain accounts and information only Dee could give her. Dee nodded, saying he would handle it, but right now, they needed to get the house in order. Pastor Campbell suggested they pray before anyone moved another inch, and the family gathered in a circle, hands linked, heads bowed. His prayer was strong, steady, and full of authority, asking for protection, clarity, and strength for the bloodline.

When the prayer ended, the room felt different — not lighter, but steadier, like the ground beneath them had stopped shaking for a moment. Aunt Jane looked at Dee and told him the next few days would decide everything. She said the block was shifting, people were choosing sides, and the family needed to be ready for the storm that was already forming.

Dee nodded, but inside, he felt the weight of leadership pressing down harder than ever. Red was moving. The block was talking. Natasha was stirring chaos. And somewhere close — too close — a snitch was feeding their enemy information.

The war hadn't started yet. But the warning shots had already been fired.

CHAPTER THREE — COREY UNDER WATCH

Corey stepped outside after the prayer circle broke, needing air, needing space, needing a moment where the walls weren't closing in on him. The block was quiet, but not the kind of quiet that brought peace — it was the kind that made your skin prickle. He walked down the steps slowly, hands in his pockets, eyes scanning the street the way Dee taught him. He wasn't born into this life the way Dee and Bobbi Jr were, but he was learning fast. Too fast. The kind of fast that meant danger was teaching the lessons.

He reached the sidewalk and looked toward the corner, noticing a car he didn't recognize — dark windows, engine running low, sitting too still. He tried to ignore it at first, telling himself he was overthinking, but something in his gut twisted. He took a few more steps, pretending to check the mailbox, pretending he wasn't watching the car. But the moment he moved, the car's headlights flicked on for half a second, like a blink. A signal. A warning. Or a message.

Corey swallowed hard and backed up slowly toward the house. He didn't want to panic, didn't want to run, didn't want to give whoever was inside that car the satisfaction of seeing fear. But his heart was pounding so loud he could hear it in his ears. When he reached the porch, he turned casually, trying to look unbothered, but the car eased forward just an inch — not enough to move down the street, just enough to let him know he was seen. Watched. Marked. He stepped inside quickly and shut the door, leaning against it as he tried to catch his breath.

Dee looked up immediately, reading Corey's face before Corey said a word. "What happened?" Dee asked, voice low, steady, ready.

Corey shook his head, trying to find the right words. "Somebody out there watching," he said. "Car on the corner. Dark windows. They blinked the lights at me." Bev gasped from the kitchen, and Kayla stood up straight, her lawyer instincts kicking in. She asked Corey if he could describe the car, but Corey shook his head again, saying it was too dark, too tinted, too intentional. Bobbi Jr's face tightened, guilt and fear mixing in his expression as he whispered that Red was starting early. Aunt Jane, still standing near her doorway, closed her eyes and murmured that the enemy always went after the one who didn't see himself as a threat yet. Corey felt that in his chest — heavy, sharp, personal.

Dee walked to the window and peeked through the blinds, but the car was gone. Just like that. No sound. No trail. No proof. Kayla said that was exactly how intimidation worked — quick, quiet, psychological. She told Corey that Red wasn't just watching him; he was testing him, seeing how he reacted, seeing if he would fold or fight. Corey felt heat rise in his chest, not fear this time, but anger — the kind that came from being targeted for something he didn't even do. He told Dee he wasn't scared, but Dee shook his head and told him fear wasn't the problem — moving wrong because of fear was.

Pastor Campbell stepped closer to Corey, placing a hand on his shoulder, telling him that when the enemy singled you out, it meant you had something he feared. Corey didn't feel powerful, didn't feel important, didn't feel like anything but a kid caught in a war he didn't start. But the pastor's words settled something inside him, something steady, something strong. Aunt Jane nodded slowly and told Corey that the bloodline wasn't just about who you were born to — it was about who you stood with when the storm came.

Corey took a deep breath and straightened his shoulders. He wasn't Dee. He wasn't Bobbi Jr. He wasn't built for the streets. But he was part of this family now, and Red had made the mistake of thinking he was the weak link. Corey looked at Dee and said, "I'm good. I'm ready." Dee studied him for a long moment, then nodded, seeing something in Corey he hadn't seen before — resolve.

But outside, somewhere in the shadows, the car that had been watching him rolled slowly down the block, unseen, unheard, choosing its next moment. Red wasn't done. And Corey had just been added to his list.

CHAPTER FOUR — RED'S CIRCLE TIGHTENS

The block felt different the next morning, like the air itself was holding its breath. Dee stepped outside before anyone else woke up, needing a moment alone with the quiet, even though the quiet didn't feel safe anymore. He scanned the street the way he always did, but today something felt off — not loud, not obvious, just... off. A trash can slightly moved from where it should've been. A car parked two houses down that hadn't been there yesterday. A curtain shifting in a window across the street. Nothing big enough to call out, but everything small enough to mean something. Red was tightening his circle, and Dee could feel it in his bones.

Inside, Corey was sitting at the table with a bowl of cereal he wasn't eating, replaying the moment from the night before when the car blinked its headlights at him. He kept telling himself he wasn't scared, but the truth sat heavy in his chest. He wasn't used to being watched. He wasn't used to being a target. He wasn't used to being part of a war he didn't start. Bev walked past him, rubbing his shoulder gently, telling him to eat something, but her voice carried worry she couldn't hide. She kept glancing out the window like she expected something to jump out of the shadows.

Kayla arrived early, dressed sharp as always, carrying her briefcase like a weapon. She sat down at the table and opened her laptop, telling Dee she had already traced two suspicious money transfers connected to Red's people. She said someone on the block was helping him move funds, someone with access, someone close enough to know the family's patterns. Dee clenched his jaw, asking her if she had a name yet, but Kayla shook her head and said she needed more time. She warned him that Red wasn't just playing street games — he was playing chess, and he was three moves ahead.

Aunt Jane shuffled into the room, leaning on her cane, her eyes sharper than her body. She told Kayla that the devil always used the weak to do his work, and whoever was talking to Red was weak in spirit. Kayla nodded respectfully, saying she agreed, but they still needed proof. Aunt Jane looked at Dee and told him to stay vigilant because the enemy was already inside the gates. Dee didn't argue — he felt it too.

Bobbi Jr came downstairs last, moving slow, shoulders heavy. He sat across from Corey and stared at the table, avoiding everyone's eyes. Corey nudged him gently, telling him they were good, they were together, they were family. Bobbi Jr nodded, but the guilt still sat on him like a weight he couldn't shake. He whispered that Red wasn't going to stop until he broke them, and Dee told him that Red wasn't breaking anything — not this family, not this house, not this bloodline.

Just as the room settled into a tense silence, a car rolled slowly down the block — the same dark sedan Corey had seen the night before. It didn't stop. It didn't speed up. It just crawled past the house like it was taking inventory. Corey stiffened. Bev gasped. Kayla snapped her laptop shut. Dee stepped toward the window, eyes narrowing. The car didn't blink its lights this time. It didn't need to. Its presence alone was a message.

Aunt Jane whispered, "He's getting closer."

Dee felt something shift inside him — not fear, not anger, but a cold, steady resolve. Red wanted to play games. Red wanted to intimidate. Red wanted to circle the block like a vulture waiting for something to die. But Dee wasn't giving him that satisfaction. He turned to the family and told them to get ready, because whatever Red was planning next wasn't going to be small.

Outside, the car reached the end of the block, paused for a long moment, then turned the corner and disappeared. But the message stayed behind, heavy and clear.
Red wasn't watching anymore. He was preparing.
    And the family had just run out of time.

.

CHAPTER FIVE — THE BLOCK STARTS CHOOSING

Word traveled fast in the 44 — faster than truth, faster than danger, faster than the family could catch their breath. By the time the sun dipped behind the rooftops, the block had already shifted. People who usually waved from their porches suddenly stayed inside. Conversations that used to happen in the open now happened behind half-closed doors. Even the kids who normally played in the street were gone, leaving the block too quiet, too still, too aware. Dee felt it the moment he stepped outside. The air had changed. The energy had changed. The loyalty had changed. Red's shadow was stretching across the 44, and people were choosing sides without saying a word.

Corey stood beside him, arms crossed, eyes scanning the street with a new kind of caution. He whispered that something felt off, and Dee nodded because he felt it too. A group of men who usually hung out near the corner store were gathered in a tight circle, talking low, glancing toward the house every few seconds. Across the street, Miss Laverne, who always brought Aunt Jane sweet tea, closed her blinds the moment she saw Dee looking. Even the dogs in the neighborhood were restless, barking at shadows that didn't move. The block wasn't just watching — it was waiting.

Inside the house, Kayla sat at the table with her laptop open, her expression sharp as she pieced together the last of the financial trail. She told Bev that once a snitch started talking, they didn't stop until they were forced to. Bev shook her head, saying she couldn't believe someone from the block would turn on them like that. Kayla corrected her gently, saying people didn't betray out of hate — they betrayed out of fear, greed, or desperation. And Red knew exactly how to use all three.

Aunt Jane sat in her chair near the window, her eyes following every movement outside. She whispered that the block was shifting, that the spirit of the neighborhood felt unsettled, that something was stirring in the air. She told Dee that when people got scared, they clung to whoever looked strongest, and right now, Red was making himself look like the one in control. Dee clenched his jaw, saying Red wasn't controlling anything, but Aunt Jane shook her head softly and told him strength wasn't always about muscle — sometimes it was about influence, fear, and timing.

Bobbi Jr paced the living room, unable to sit still, feeling the weight of everything pressing down on him. He kept saying he didn't want the block turning against them because of him. Corey stepped inside and told him it wasn't about him — it was about Red trying to isolate the family, trying to make them feel alone, trying to make them doubt their own people. Bobbi Jr nodded, but the guilt still clung to him like a shadow he couldn't outrun.

As night settled in, the block grew even quieter. A car rolled slowly past the house, not the same one from before, but the same energy — slow, deliberate, watching. Dee stepped onto the porch, staring it down until it turned the corner. He didn't flinch. He didn't blink. He wanted whoever was inside to know he saw them too. Corey stood behind him, whispering that the block wasn't with them anymore. Dee shook his head and said the block didn't have to be with them — the family just had to be with each other.

Aunt Jane called out from inside, her voice steady but heavy. She told Dee that the block choosing sides wasn't the real danger — the real danger was the moment the snitch realized the family knew. She said betrayal always came with consequences, and the snitch would feel the pressure long before Red did. Kayla looked up from her laptop and said Aunt Jane was right — the snitch was already panicking. She could see it in the financial patterns, the rushed transfers, the sudden silence.

Dee stepped back inside and closed the door, locking it with a slow, deliberate click. He looked around the room at the people he loved — tired, scared, angry, but still standing. He told them the block could choose whatever side it wanted, but the family wasn't breaking. Not now. Not ever.

Outside, the streetlights flickered, one by one, like the block itself was holding its breath.

The storm was coming. And the 44 was already shifting under its weight.

CHAPTER SIX — PASTOR CAMPBELL'S VISIT

Pastor Campbell stayed longer than he planned, sensing the heaviness sitting in the house like a weight no one could lift. He moved quietly through the living room, his presence steady, calm, and grounding in a way the family desperately needed. Dee sat across from him, elbows on his knees, staring at the floor as if the answers were hidden in the wood grain. The pastor watched him for a moment before speaking, telling him that leadership wasn't about being fearless — it was about standing firm even when fear tried to take over. Dee didn't respond right away. He just exhaled slowly, rubbing the back of his neck, admitting that everything felt like it was closing in at once — Red circling the block, the snitch feeding him information, Natasha stirring chaos, and the family looking to him for direction he wasn't sure he had.

Pastor Campbell leaned back in his chair, folding his hands, saying the enemy always attacked the head first because if the head fell, the body followed. He told Dee that Red wasn't just after the family physically — he was after their unity, their peace, their foundation. Dee nodded, feeling the truth of those words settle deep in his chest. He said he could handle Red coming for him, but he couldn't handle Red coming for the people he loved. The pastor told him that was exactly why Red was doing it — because he knew Dee's heart, and he knew the family was his weakness and his strength at the same time.

Bev walked in with a tray of tea, her hands still trembling slightly from everything that had happened. She set the tray down and sat beside Dee, leaning into him without saying a word. Pastor Campbell looked at her gently and told her she carried the weight of the house in ways no one else saw. Bev wiped her eyes and said she was tired — tired of the fear, tired of the threats, tired of feeling like the block she grew up on was turning into a battlefield. The pastor nodded and told her that weariness was natural, but surrender wasn't an option. He reminded her that storms didn't last forever, even when they felt endless.

Aunt Jane shuffled into the room, her steps slow but her spirit strong. She sat beside the pastor and told him she felt something shifting in the air — something spiritual, something heavy, something that wasn't just about Red or the streets. She said she felt a darkness trying to settle over the family, trying to break them from the inside out. Pastor Campbell nodded, saying he felt it too, and that was why he came. He said he woke up with a stirring in his spirit, a warning that the family needed covering, protection, and clarity before the next move came.

Corey and Bobbi Jr joined them, sitting quietly on the couch, listening. The pastor looked at Corey and told him he was stepping into a role he didn't ask for but was chosen for. Corey swallowed hard, unsure what that meant, but the pastor told him he had a strength he didn't recognize yet — a strength the enemy saw before he did. Bobbi Jr lowered his head, guilt still clinging to him, but Pastor Campbell told him guilt was a chain the enemy used to keep him from rising. He said Bobbi Jr had a purpose beyond his mistakes, and Red knew that too.

The pastor stood and asked everyone to join hands. The family formed a circle — tired, shaken, but connected. His prayer filled the room, strong and steady, asking for protection over the house, clarity over their decisions, and strength for the battles ahead. He prayed against confusion, against betrayal, against fear. He prayed for unity, for wisdom, for peace. And as he prayed, the air in the room shifted — not lighter, but steadier, like the foundation beneath them had been reinforced.

When the prayer ended, Pastor Campbell looked at Dee and told him the next few days would test everything — their loyalty, their faith, their strength, and their legacy. He said the enemy was moving fast, but God was moving faster. Dee nodded, feeling something settle inside him — not relief, but resolve.

As the pastor gathered his things and prepared to leave, he paused at the door and looked back at the family. He told them storms didn't come to destroy — they came to reveal what was built to last. Then he stepped outside into the quiet night, leaving the family with a sense of calm they hadn't felt in days.

But the moment the door closed, a car rolled slowly past the house, its engine low, its windows dark, its presence unmistakable.

The storm wasn't over. It was just beginning.

CHAPTER SEVEN — KAYLA STEPS IN

Kayla didn't go home that night. She stayed in her car outside the house, laptop open, eyes burning from staring at screens for too long, but her mind sharper than ever. She knew Red wasn't sloppy — he didn't leave trails unless he wanted someone to find them. That meant the snitch wasn't just feeding him information; they were helping him build something bigger. She traced another transfer, smaller than the last, but timed perfectly with the moment the dark sedan rolled past the house earlier. It wasn't coincidence. It was coordination. Kayla leaned back in her seat, exhaling slowly as the truth settled in — the snitch wasn't scared. They were confident. Too confident. And confidence meant they believed Red could protect them.

Inside the house, Dee paced the living room while Corey sat on the couch, replaying the moment the car watched him. Bev moved quietly through the kitchen, wiping down counters that were already clean, trying to keep her hands busy so her mind wouldn't spiral. Aunt Jane sat in her chair near the window, watching the street with the same intensity she used when she used to grade papers, her spirit alert, her intuition sharper than any camera. Bobbi Jr sat on the floor with his back against the wall, knees pulled up, staring at the doorway like he expected Red to walk through it at any moment. The house felt like a pressure cooker — silent, tense, waiting for something to break.

Kayla finally came inside, closing the door behind her with a soft click that made everyone look up. She didn't sit. She didn't ease into the conversation. She stood in the center of the room and told them she found something new — something worse. She explained that the snitch wasn't just sending information; they were receiving instructions.

Red was using them like a chess piece, moving them around the block to test the family's reactions. She said the snitch had been near the house three times in the last twenty-four hours, each time right before Red's car appeared. Corey's stomach dropped as he realized the snitch had probably been watching him too.

Dee asked Kayla if she knew who it was yet, but she shook her head, saying she was close, but she needed one more piece — one more transfer, one more message, one more slip-up. Aunt Jane told her the truth would reveal itself soon because lies never stayed hidden long in the 44. Kayla nodded, saying she agreed, but they needed to be ready for what happened when the truth came out. She warned them that snitches didn't confess — they panicked. And panicked people were dangerous.

Bev sat down slowly, her voice trembling as she asked why someone from their own block would turn on them. Kayla told her betrayal didn't always come from hate — sometimes it came from fear, sometimes from greed, sometimes from jealousy. She said Red knew how to find the cracks in people and pry them open. Dee clenched his jaw, saying he didn't care what the reason was — once he knew who it was, it was over. Aunt Jane looked at him sharply and told him not to let anger make his decisions. She said anger clouded judgment, and judgment was the only thing keeping them alive right now.

Kayla closed her laptop and told them she needed to step out for a moment to make a call. She walked onto the porch, the night air cool against her skin, and dialed a number she rarely used — a contact who owed her a favor, someone who could access records she couldn't. As the phone rang, she looked down the block and saw a porch light flicker on, then off, then on again. A signal. A pattern. A warning. She narrowed her eyes, realizing the snitch wasn't hiding anymore. They were watching the house openly now, bold enough to send signals in plain sight.

When her contact answered, Kayla spoke quickly, asking for the information she needed. She hung up and stepped back inside, her expression tight. She told the family she would have the name by morning. Dee nodded, but the tension in his shoulders didn't ease. Corey swallowed hard, feeling the weight of the night pressing down on him. Bev whispered a prayer under her breath. Aunt Jane closed her eyes, sensing the shift in the air.

The block wasn't just choosing sides anymore. It was preparing for war.
And the snitch was already moving their next piece.

CHAPTER EIGHT — NATASHA'S ACCUSATION

Natasha showed up the next morning like she had been waiting for the sun to rise just so she could cause trouble. Dee was barely awake, standing in the kitchen with a cup of coffee he hadn't even tasted yet, when the knock hit the door — sharp, impatient, and full of attitude. Bev looked up from the stove, already annoyed, already knowing who it was. Corey muttered under his breath, and Aunt Jane sighed like she felt the disturbance before the door even opened. Dee set his cup down and walked to the front, bracing himself, because Natasha never came quietly.

The moment he opened the door, she pushed past him like she lived there, her perfume loud, her energy louder. She stood in the middle of the living room with her hands on her hips, staring at everyone like they were the ones who owed her something. Dee told her she needed to leave, but Natasha shook her head and said she wasn't going anywhere until they talked. Bev stepped forward, her voice sharp as she asked what Natasha wanted now. Natasha lifted her chin and said she came to make things clear — she wasn't backing down, she wasn't going away, and she wasn't letting Dee pretend the situation didn't exist.

Dee rubbed his forehead, already exhausted, telling her again that the baby wasn't his. Natasha rolled her eyes dramatically, saying men always denied it first, but she wasn't stupid and she wasn't scared. She said she had receipts, she had dates, she had everything she needed to prove her point. Corey scoffed from the couch, whispering that she had everything except the truth. Natasha snapped her head toward him, telling him to stay out of grown folks' business. Corey stood up, ready to say something back, but Aunt Jane raised her hand gently, stopping him with a look that carried more authority than any shout.

Natasha turned back to Dee, her voice rising as she said she wasn't going to be ignored, and if he didn't want to deal with her, she would go straight to Cece. The room tensed instantly. Bev stepped forward, her voice low and dangerous, telling Natasha she wasn't dragging Cece into her mess. Natasha smirked, saying she would talk to whoever she needed to talk to, because she wasn't about to let Dee play her like she was stupid. Dee told her again, firmly this time, that the baby wasn't his and she needed to stop using Cece's name like a weapon.

Kayla walked in from the hallway just in time to hear the last part, her expression unimpressed as she asked if Natasha had any actual evidence or if she was just here to cause chaos. Natasha glared at her, saying she didn't need a lawyer to tell her what she already knew. Kayla crossed her arms and told her that if she was going to make accusations, she needed proof — real proof — not drama. Natasha's face twisted, and she said she didn't owe anyone proof, she owed Dee responsibility. Aunt Jane shook her head slowly, telling Natasha that lies had a way of coming back on the liar, and she needed to be careful about the seeds she was planting.

Natasha's eyes flickered, just for a moment, like Aunt Jane's words hit deeper than she wanted to admit. But she recovered quickly, flipping her hair and saying she wasn't scared of anybody in this house. She said she would be back with whatever she needed to bring, and when she did, Dee better be ready. Then she stormed out, slamming the door so hard the walls shook.
The house fell silent for a long moment. Bev exhaled loudly, saying she was tired of Natasha's games. Corey

shook his head, saying Natasha picked the worst possible time to start drama. Kayla sat down at the table, opening her laptop again, saying Natasha wasn't the real problem — she was a distraction. And distractions were dangerous when the enemy was already moving.

Aunt Jane looked at Dee with eyes full of warning. She told him Natasha wasn't acting alone — she was being pushed by something, stirred by something, used by something. She said the enemy didn't always come with guns or threats. Sometimes he came with confusion. Sometimes he came with lies. Sometimes he came wearing perfume and attitude.

Dee sat down slowly, rubbing his temples, feeling the weight of everything pressing down at once — Red circling the block, the snitch feeding him information, and now Natasha threatening to drag Cece into a storm she didn't deserve

The family didn't need another enemy. But Natasha had just made herself one.

CHAPTER NINE — BEV DRAWS THE LINE

Bev had been quiet all morning, moving through the house with a tight jaw and a stare that warned everyone not to test her. She washed dishes that were already clean, wiped counters that didn't need wiping, and kept glancing out the window like she was waiting for something — or someone — to push her too far. The block had been shifting for days, Natasha had stormed in with her lies, and Red's people were circling like vultures. Bev felt all of it pressing on her chest, squeezing her patience thin. She wasn't scared — she was fed up. And Bev fed up was a different kind of storm.

She finally sat down at the table, exhaling hard as she rubbed her temples. Corey walked in and asked if she was okay, but Bev waved him off, saying she was tired of everybody acting like the family was supposed to just sit back and take whatever came their way. She said the block was acting funny, people were whispering, and Natasha was running around talking like she had power she didn't earn. Corey sat across from her, nodding slowly, telling her he felt it too — the shift, the tension, the eyes watching them like they were the problem instead of the ones being hunted.

Bev leaned back in her chair, her voice low but sharp as she said she wasn't about to let Natasha drag Cece into anything. She said Cece had her own life, her own peace, her own world, and she wasn't letting some girl with too much attitude and not enough truth pull her name into mess. Aunt Jane, listening from her chair near the window, nodded and told Bev that protecting peace was just as important as protecting family. Bev agreed, saying she didn't care what Natasha claimed — she wasn't letting lies take root in her house.

Kayla walked in with her laptop tucked under her arm, catching the tail end of the conversation. She told Bev she understood the frustration, but Natasha wasn't the real threat — she was noise. The real danger was the snitch feeding Red information, the one who knew their movements, their routines, their vulnerabilities. Bev shook her head, saying she didn't care who the snitch was — once they found out, she wanted them gone. Kayla raised an eyebrow, reminding her that snitches didn't always leave quietly. Bev didn't flinch. She said she didn't care how they left, as long as they did.

Dee walked in next, overhearing enough to know Bev was reaching her breaking point. He sat beside her, placing a hand on her knee, telling her he understood the pressure she was under. Bev looked at him, eyes sharp, saying she wasn't scared of Red, she wasn't scared of Natasha, and she wasn't scared of whoever was talking. What she was scared of was the family falling apart from the inside. Dee nodded, knowing she was right — the danger outside wasn't half as deadly as the cracks forming inside the house.

Aunt Jane cleared her throat softly, drawing everyone's attention. She told Bev that strength didn't always look like fighting — sometimes it looked like standing firm, refusing to be moved, refusing to let fear or lies dictate the atmosphere of the home. Bev took a deep breath, letting the words settle. She said she wasn't trying to fight — she was trying to protect. And she wasn't about to let anyone, not Red, not Natasha, not the snitch, tear apart what she and Dee had built.

Just then, a loud knock hit the door — not frantic, not

threatening, but bold. Bev stood up before anyone else could move, wiping her hands on her jeans as she walked toward the door with a determination that made Corey whisper, "Oh boy." Dee tried to stop her, but Bev shook her head, saying she had it. She opened the door slowly, ready for anything — except what she saw.

It wasn't Red. It wasn't Natasha. It wasn't the snitch.
It was someone from the block — someone who never came to the house, someone who usually kept their distance, someone who looked nervous just standing there. They shifted from foot to foot, glancing over their shoulder before whispering that they needed to talk to Dee. Bev narrowed her eyes, stepping aside just enough to let them in, but not enough to make them comfortable.

The moment they crossed the threshold, the air in the room changed. Aunt Jane sat up straighter. Corey moved closer. Kayla opened her laptop. Dee stood tall .

Bev folded her arms, her voice steady and cold as she said, "Whoever you came to talk about... you better tell the truth." Because Bev wasn't playing anymore. And the block was about to feel it.
nine text here. Insert chapter nine text here.

CHAPTER TEN — COREY'S FIRST TEST

Corey couldn't shake the feeling that the block was breathing down his neck. Every time he stepped outside, he felt eyes on him — not the usual neighborhood glances, but the kind that lingered too long, the kind that carried weight, the kind that made his stomach tighten. He tried to ignore it, tried to act normal, but the tension sat on his shoulders like a backpack full of bricks. He walked down the steps that afternoon, telling himself he was just going to the corner store, just grabbing a drink, just doing something simple. But nothing in the 44 was simple anymore.

As he walked down the sidewalk, he noticed two men standing near the alley — men he'd seen before but never paid attention to. Today, they were paying attention to him. One of them nodded in his direction, slow and deliberate, like he was acknowledging something Corey didn't understand yet. Corey kept walking, pretending he didn't see it, pretending he wasn't bothered, pretending he wasn't replaying the moment the dark sedan blinked its headlights at him. He reached the store, grabbed a bottle of water, and stepped back outside — only to find the same two men now standing closer, leaning against a car that hadn't been there five minutes ago.

Corey's heart thumped hard, but he kept his face straight. He walked past them, but one of the men called out, asking if he was "Dee's little protégé." Corey stopped, turning slowly, trying to read their intentions. The man smirked, saying Red had been asking about him, saying Red liked to know who was being groomed, saying Red liked to know who was stepping into roles they didn't earn. Corey felt heat rise in his chest, but he didn't react. He remembered what Dee told him — reacting wrong was how you got caught slipping.

The second man stepped forward, circling Corey like he was sizing him up. He said the block was changing, lines were being drawn, and Corey needed to decide which side he was on. Corey swallowed hard, saying he was with his family. The man laughed, saying family didn't mean much when bullets started flying. Corey clenched his fists, but he kept his voice steady, saying he wasn't scared. The man leaned in close, whispering that fear wasn't the problem — being unprepared was.

Before Corey could respond, a car rolled slowly down the street — not Red's, but one of his people. The window slid down just enough for Corey to see a pair of eyes watching him, studying him, testing him. The car didn't stop. It didn't speak. It just crawled past, slow and intentional, like it was marking him. The two men stepped back, smirking, telling Corey they'd be seeing him around. Then they walked off, disappearing into the alley like shadows.

Corey stood frozen for a moment, his heart pounding so hard he could feel it in his throat. He turned and walked back toward the house, faster this time, his mind racing. He didn't want to look scared, but he felt something he hadn't felt before — not fear, but awareness. Red wasn't just watching him. Red was testing him. Red was trying to see if he would fold, if he would panic, if he would run.

When Corey stepped back inside, Dee looked up immediately, reading everything on his face. Corey told him what happened, every detail, every word, every look. Dee listened quietly, his jaw tightening with each sentence. When Corey finished, Dee placed a hand on his shoulder and told him this was the first test — the first of many — and Corey passed because he didn't fold. Corey exhaled shakily, asking if Red was coming for him. Dee shook his head and said Red wasn't coming for Corey — he was coming for the family, and Corey was just the easiest one to reach.

Aunt Jane, listening from her chair, told Corey that the enemy always went after the ones who didn't know their own strength yet. She said Corey had more power than he realized, and Red saw it before he did. Corey sat down slowly, letting her words settle in his chest like a weight and a shield at the same time.

Bev walked over and hugged him, her voice trembling as she told him she didn't want him going anywhere alone anymore. Corey nodded, not arguing, not pretending to be brave. He felt the danger now — real, close, personal.

Kayla closed her laptop and said Corey's encounter confirmed something — Red wasn't just circling. He was recruiting. Testing. Pressuring. And the snitch was helping him choose targets.

Corey looked around the room, seeing the fear, the anger, the resolve. He realized something in that moment — he wasn't just part of the family anymore.
He was part of the war.

CHAPTER ELEVEN — Bobbi Jr's Shadow

Bobbi Jr had been quiet all morning, moving through the house like a ghost drifting from room to room. He barely spoke, barely ate, barely looked anyone in the eye. The weight of everything — Red circling the block, the snitch feeding him information, Corey being tested, Natasha stirring chaos — sat on his shoulders heavier than anyone else realized. He felt responsible for all of it, even the parts that had nothing to do with him. Guilt had wrapped itself around him like a shadow he couldn't outrun, and every time he tried to shake it, it clung tighter.

He sat on the edge of the couch, elbows on his knees, staring at the floor as if the answers were hidden in the cracks. Corey walked in and sat beside him, nudging him gently, telling him he didn't have to carry everything alone. Bobbi Jr didn't respond. He just swallowed hard, his voice barely above a whisper as he said he felt like everything that was happening was his fault — the threats, the fear, the block turning cold. Corey shook his head, telling him Red was the problem, not him. But Bobbi Jr didn't believe it. He said Red wouldn't be circling the block if it weren't for him. Red wouldn't be testing Corey. Red wouldn't be watching the house. Red wouldn't be tightening his grip on the 44.

Bev overheard the last part and walked over, sitting on the arm of the couch, telling Bobbi Jr he wasn't the cause of Red's evil — Red was who he was long before any of this started. She told him he couldn't blame himself for a man who thrived on chaos. But Bobbi Jr shook his head again, saying he should've handled things differently, should've seen the danger coming, should've protected the family better. His voice cracked, and Bev's heart broke a little. She reached out and squeezed his shoulder, telling him guilt was a liar, and he needed to stop letting it speak louder than the truth.

Aunt Jane shuffled into the room, her presence soft but commanding. She sat across from Bobbi Jr and told him she could feel the heaviness sitting on him, the kind that didn't come from the outside but from the inside. She said guilt was a trap the enemy used to keep strong men weak, and Bobbi Jr had too much purpose to let guilt choke him. Bobbi Jr looked up at her, eyes glassy, asking how he was supposed to move forward when everything around him was falling apart. Aunt Jane leaned forward, her voice steady, telling him he didn't move forward alone — he moved with family, with faith, with strength he didn't even know he had yet.

Kayla walked in next, closing her laptop as she sat on the coffee table in front of him. She told him she understood pressure — the kind that made you feel like every wrong move would break everything. She said she understood guilt too — the kind that whispered lies in your ear until you believed them. But she told him something else: guilt didn't fix anything. Action did. And right now, the family needed him present, not drowning in what-ifs.

Dee finally stepped into the room, leaning against the doorway, watching his son with a mixture of worry and pride. He walked over and sat beside him, placing a hand on his back. He told Bobbi Jr that he wasn't alone, that the family wasn't blaming him, and that Red wasn't circling because of him — Red was circling because he was scared of what the family could become if they stayed united. Bobbi Jr looked at him, eyes full of doubt, but Dee held his gaze and told him he needed to stop carrying weight that didn't belong to him.

Just then, a car rolled slowly past the house — again. The same slow crawl, the same dark windows, the same silent message. Bobbi Jr stiffened, his breath catching in his chest. Corey stood up, moving toward the window. Dee followed, jaw tightening. Aunt Jane whispered a prayer under her breath. Kayla grabbed her laptop. Bev closed her eyes, steadying herself.

Bobbi Jr stood up slowly, his hands shaking, but something in his expression had shifted — not fear, not guilt, but resolve. He said he was done hiding in the shadows. He said he was done letting Red control his mind. He said he was done letting guilt speak louder than truth. Aunt Jane nodded, her eyes softening. "That's it, baby," she whispered. "Stand up." The car turned the corner and disappeared, but the moment stayed heavy in the room. Bobbi Jr wasn't healed. He wasn't whole. But he was standing. And sometimes, in the middle of a war, that was the first victory.

CHAPTER TWELVE — The Snitch on the Block

Kayla barely slept. She spent the entire night hunched over her laptop at the dining table, her eyes burning, her fingers moving fast, her mind sharper than the exhaustion pulling at her. The house was quiet except for the soft hum of the refrigerator and the occasional creak of the floorboards as Aunt Jane moved through her room. Everyone else was asleep, but Kayla couldn't rest until she had the truth. She knew she was close — too close — and the closer she got, the more the numbers started lining up like puzzle pieces snapping into place.

Just after sunrise, her phone buzzed with a message from the contact she'd called the night before. Kayla opened it, scanned the information, and froze. Her breath caught in her chest as she stared at the name on the screen. It wasn't who she expected. It wasn't who anyone expected. It wasn't someone loud, messy, or reckless. It was someone quiet. Someone familiar. Someone who blended into the block so well that no one ever looked twice. Someone who had been in their house more than once. Someone who smiled in their faces.

Kayla closed her laptop slowly, her heart pounding as she stood up and walked toward the living room. Dee was already awake, sitting on the couch with his elbows on his knees, staring at the floor like he'd been waiting for something to break. Corey walked in behind him, rubbing sleep from his eyes. Bev came from the kitchen with a cup of coffee she didn't even sip. Aunt Jane stepped out of her room, leaning on her cane, her spirit alert. Bobbi Jr hovered near the hallway, tense and restless.

Kayla didn't sit. She didn't ease into it. She stood in front of them and said she had the name. The room went still. Dee looked up slowly, his voice low as he asked who it was. Kayla hesitated for the first time since she started the investigation. She took a breath, steadying herself, then said the name out loud.

The reaction was instant. Bev gasped, her hand flying to her chest. Corey's eyes widened in disbelief. Bobbi Jr cursed under his breath, pacing in a tight circle. Aunt Jane closed her eyes, whispering something soft and heavy. Dee didn't move at first. He just stared at Kayla like he needed her to say it again, like he needed to make sure he heard it right. When she repeated it, his jaw tightened, and something cold settled in his expression.

Kayla explained everything — the transfers, the timing, the messages, the location pings. She said the snitch had been feeding Red information for weeks, maybe longer. She said the snitch wasn't just talking — they were coordinating. They were helping Red choose targets. They were helping him move money. They were helping him tighten his circle around the family. Bev shook her head, saying she couldn't believe it. She said she trusted that person. She said she let them in her house. Aunt Jane opened her eyes and said betrayal always came from someone close enough to hurt you. Corey whispered that he knew something felt off. Bobbi Jr punched the wall lightly, not enough to break anything, but enough to release the frustration boiling inside him.

Dee finally stood up, his voice low and steady as he asked Kayla if she was sure. Kayla nodded without hesitation. She said she triple-checked everything. She said there was no doubt. She said the snitch wasn't hiding anymore — they were getting sloppy, panicked, making mistakes. And mistakes were how she caught them.

Aunt Jane stepped forward, her voice soft but strong, saying the truth always came to light, even when darkness tried to bury it. She told Dee that what he did next would determine everything — not just for the family, but for the block. Dee nodded slowly, his eyes dark with resolve. He said he wasn't going to act out of anger. He wasn't going to act out of fear. He was going to act out of protection.

Because now that they knew who the snitch was, the war had officially changed. And the block would never be the same.

CHAPTER THIRTEEN — Red Sends His Warning

The block was too quiet that night — the kind of quiet that didn't feel like peace but like something holding its breath. Dee felt it the moment he stepped onto the porch. The air was heavy, thick, charged with something he couldn't name but recognized instantly. Danger had a sound, a smell, a weight. And tonight, it was sitting on the 44 like a storm cloud waiting to break. Corey stood beside him, arms crossed, eyes scanning the street the way Dee taught him, but even he could feel it — the shift, the tension, the wrongness.

Inside, Kayla was at the table with her laptop open, preparing the evidence she'd gathered about the snitch. Bev moved through the kitchen quietly, her nerves stretched thin. Aunt Jane sat near the window, watching the street with a stillness that came from knowing something was coming. Bobbi Jr paced the living room, unable to sit still, unable to shake the feeling that the night was about to turn.

Then it happened.
A single car rolled down the block — slow, deliberate, silent except for the low hum of its engine. It wasn't the sedan that had been watching them before. This one was different. Bigger. Darker. More intentional. Dee straightened, his jaw tightening as the car approached the house. Corey whispered that something felt wrong, and Dee nodded without taking his eyes off the vehicle.

The car didn't stop. It didn't speed up. It just crawled past the house like it was studying every brick, every window, every shadow. Then, as it reached the middle of the block, the back window slid down just an inch —

enough for a hand to appear. A gloved hand. Holding something small. Something metallic. Something that glinted under the streetlight. A bullet. Not fired. Not aimed. Just shown. A message. The hand held it up for a long moment, letting the meaning sink in, letting the threat settle into the air like smoke. Then the window slid back up, and the car continued down the street, turning the corner without a sound.

Corey exhaled shakily, whispering that Red was playing games. Dee shook his head, saying this wasn't a game — this was a warning. A promise. A declaration. Red wasn't hiding anymore. He wanted them to know he was close. He wanted them to feel him breathing down their necks. He wanted them to understand that the next move would not be subtle.

Inside the house, Kayla looked up from her laptop, sensing the shift. Bev rushed to the window, her hand covering her mouth as she saw the car disappear. Aunt Jane closed her eyes, whispering a prayer that sounded more like a shield than a plea. Bobbi Jr froze in the middle of the room, his breath catching in his chest as the reality of the moment hit him.

Dee stepped back inside, locking the door with a slow, deliberate click. He told the family what happened, and the room fell into a heavy silence. Kayla said Red was escalating. Bev said she felt sick. Corey said he wasn't scared, but his voice trembled just enough for Aunt Jane to reach out and touch his hand. Bobbi Jr whispered that Red was coming for them, and Dee told him Red had already arrived.

Aunt Jane lifted her head, her voice steady as she said the

enemy always announced himself before he attacked — not out of arrogance, but out of strategy. She said Red wanted them rattled. Wanted them shaken. Wanted them divided. Dee nodded, saying Red wasn't getting that satisfaction.

But even as he said it, the weight of the moment pressed down on the room.
The bullet wasn't a threat. It was a countdown.
And the family knew the clock had just started ticking.

Bonus- The Block Starts Whispering

By the next morning, the 44 felt different — not just tense, not just quiet, but watchful. The kind of watchful that made the hairs on the back of your neck stand up. Word had already started spreading, even though the family hadn't said a thing. The block always knew when something was brewing. People didn't need details; they could feel the shift in the air. And today, the air felt thick with whispers, suspicion, and something darker — anticipation.

Dee stepped outside early, standing on the porch with his arms crossed as he scanned the street. He could feel eyes on him from behind curtains, from porches, from cars parked too long in the same spot. Folks who normally waved kept their distance. Folks who normally spoke kept their mouths shut. Folks who normally minded their business suddenly seemed too interested. The block wasn't neutral anymore. It was choosing. Watching. Waiting.

Inside, Kayla sat at the table with her laptop open, the snitch's name highlighted on the screen like a wound. She didn't say it out loud again — she didn't need to. The family had heard it, felt it, absorbed it. Bev moved around the kitchen with a tight jaw, slamming cabinets harder than necessary, muttering under her breath about betrayal and how she should've trusted her instincts. Corey sat on the couch, bouncing his knee, replaying every interaction he'd ever had with the snitch, trying to figure out how he missed the signs. Bobbi Jr paced the hallway, restless, angry, and ready for answers.

Aunt Jane sat in her chair near the window, her eyes

narrowed as she watched the block with a knowing expression. She told the family that the truth had cracked something open — not just inside the house, but outside too. She said the block could feel the shift, even if they didn't know the details. She said people were whispering because they sensed something was coming, something big, something that would change the 44 for good.

Dee came back inside, closing the door slowly, his face tight with resolve. He told the family they needed to move carefully. He said confronting the snitch wasn't just about calling them out — it was about understanding why they did it, who else they were connected to, and what Red had promised them. Kayla nodded, saying the snitch wasn't acting alone. She said the financial patterns showed coordination, not desperation. She said the snitch believed Red could protect them — or reward them.

Bev scoffed, saying Red couldn't protect anybody from what was coming. Aunt Jane looked at her sharply and said anger was understandable, but they needed clarity, not chaos. She told them the enemy wanted them emotional, reactive, reckless. She said they needed to stay grounded, stay united, stay focused.

Just then, a knock hit the door — soft, hesitant, almost scared. The family froze. Dee motioned for everyone to stay back as he approached the door slowly. When he opened it, a young boy from the block stood there, shifting nervously from foot to foot. He said he had a message — not from Red, but from someone who didn't want to be seen talking to the family. Someone who said the snitch was scared. Someone who said the snitch knew the family knew. Someone who said the snitch was planning to run.

The room shifted instantly.

Kayla stood up, her expression sharp. Corey's jaw clenched. Bev whispered, "Coward." Bobbi Jr stepped forward, asking where the snitch was now. The boy shrugged, saying he didn't know — only that the snitch had been seen packing a bag, moving fast, looking over their shoulder like they expected someone to come for them.

Aunt Jane closed her eyes, whispering that the truth always made the guilty flee. Dee thanked the boy and closed the door, turning back to the family with a look that said everything without saying a word.

The snitch wasn't waiting for confrontation. They were running from it.
And that meant one thing — Red had already told them the storm was coming.

CHAPTER FOURTEEN — The Block Speaks

The man stood just inside the doorway, shifting nervously from foot to foot, his eyes darting around the room like he expected someone to burst in behind him. Bev crossed her arms, watching him with a stare sharp enough to cut through excuses. Dee stepped forward slowly, not aggressive, but firm, letting the man know he wasn't here for games. Corey hovered near the hallway, alert, while Bobbi Jr leaned against the wall, jaw tight. Aunt Jane sat in her chair near the window, her presence steady, her spirit already reading the truth beneath the man's trembling voice.

He finally spoke, his words low and shaky as he said the block wasn't the same anymore. He said people were scared — not just of Red, but of what Red was planning. He said folks were whispering, choosing sides, distancing themselves from the family because they didn't want to get caught in the crossfire. Bev's eyes narrowed, her voice sharp as she asked why he came now, why he waited until things got this bad. The man swallowed hard and said he didn't want trouble, didn't want to be involved, didn't want to pick a side — but Red wasn't giving people choices anymore.

Kayla stepped closer, her tone calm but cutting as she asked him what Red was doing. The man hesitated, glancing toward the window like he feared being seen. He said Red had been sending people door to door, not openly, not loudly, but quietly — checking who was loyal, who was scared, who could be influenced. He said Red was promising protection to anyone who stayed out of the family's business, and promising consequences to anyone who didn't. Corey muttered under his breath that Red was playing psychological warfare. Dee didn't disagree.

The man continued, saying Red had eyes everywhere — on the corners, in the alleys, behind curtains. He said the block wasn't ignoring the family out of hate; they were doing it out of survival. Bev shook her head, hurt flashing across her face as she whispered that survival shouldn't mean betrayal. Aunt Jane lifted her chin, telling her softly that fear made people forget who they were. The man nodded quickly, saying that was exactly what was happening — people were forgetting themselves, forgetting their loyalty, forgetting the truth.

Kayla asked him directly if he knew who the snitch was. The man froze, his eyes widening, his breath catching. He said he didn't know names, but he knew someone was talking — someone close, someone trusted, someone who moved around the block without raising suspicion. He said Red bragged about having someone "inside," someone who made things easy. Dee's jaw tightened, but he stayed silent, letting the man speak.

Then the man said something that made the room shift.

He said Red wasn't just planning to intimidate anymore — he was planning to strike. Not today. Not tomorrow. But soon. He said Red wanted the block to see it, wanted the block to understand who held the power, wanted the block to know the family wasn't untouchable. Corey felt his stomach drop. Bobbi Jr's fists clenched. Bev whispered a prayer under her breath. Kayla's expression hardened.

Aunt Jane leaned forward, her voice steady as she asked the man why he came to them now. He swallowed again, his voice cracking as he said he didn't want blood on his hands. He said he couldn't sleep knowing something was coming and staying silent would make him part of it. He said he didn't want to be a coward anymore.

Dee nodded slowly, telling him he did the right thing by coming. But the man shook his head, saying it wasn't bravery — it was fear. Fear of what Red would do. Fear of what the family might do. Fear of being caught in the middle. He said he was leaving the block for a while, staying with family across town until things calmed down. He said he didn't want to be here when the storm hit.

Bev stepped aside, letting him leave, but her eyes followed him until he disappeared down the street. The moment the door closed, the house fell into a heavy silence. Kayla opened her laptop, her fingers moving fast. Corey paced. Bobbi Jr stared at the floor. Aunt Jane whispered that the truth had finally spoken.

Dee stood in the center of the room, his voice low and steady as he said, "Red's not waiting anymore."

And everyone in the room felt it — the shift, the warning, the countdown.

The storm wasn't coming. It was already here.

CHAPTER FIFTEEN — The Block Turns Cold

The block felt colder than usual the next morning, the kind of cold that didn't come from the weather but from people pulling back, pulling away, pulling into themselves. Dee stepped outside before anyone else woke up, standing on the porch with his hands in his pockets, staring at the street that suddenly felt unfamiliar. The same houses were there, the same cracked sidewalks, the same leaning streetlights — but the energy had shifted. Neighbors who used to wave now closed their doors. Cars that usually drove by without a thought now slowed down just enough to watch. The block wasn't just quiet. It was distant. Suspicious. Divided.

Corey joined him on the porch, rubbing his arms against the morning chill. He whispered that the block didn't feel like home anymore, and Dee nodded, saying the block wasn't choosing sides — it had already chosen. Corey swallowed hard, asking if Red had that much influence. Dee didn't answer right away. He just stared at the corner where the dark sedan had appeared night after night, feeling the weight of leadership pressing down on him. He finally said Red didn't need influence — he needed fear. And fear was spreading faster than truth.

Inside, Bev moved through the kitchen with a heaviness she couldn't shake. She kept glancing out the window, watching the neighbors pretend not to look at the house. She whispered to herself that she didn't recognize the block anymore. Aunt Jane shuffled in behind her, leaning on her cane, telling her that fear made people act strange, made them forget loyalty, made them forget who stood by them when times were good. Bev nodded, but her eyes were sharp, her spirit restless. She said she wasn't scared — she was angry. Angry that the block she grew up on was turning its back on them. Angry that Red had poisoned the air. Angry that betrayal had come from someone they trusted.

Kayla sat at the dining table with her laptop open, reviewing the evidence again, making sure there were no mistakes. She told Dee that the snitch wasn't just feeding Red information — they were helping him manipulate the block. She said the snitch had been spreading rumors, planting seeds, twisting stories to make the family look unstable, dangerous, unpredictable. Dee clenched his jaw, saying he didn't care what the block thought — he cared about keeping his family safe. Kayla nodded, but she warned him that perception mattered. If the block believed Red had control, they would act like it.

Bobbi Jr walked into the room, shoulders tense, eyes tired. He said he heard people talking outside — whispering, pointing, acting like the family was the problem. Corey stepped in behind him, saying he heard it too. Aunt Jane told them not to let whispers shake them. She said whispers were weak, and weak people hid behind noise. But even as she spoke, the heaviness in the room didn't lift.

Just then, a group of neighbors walked past the house — people who used to stop and chat, people who used to ask about the kids, people who used to bring plates during holidays. Today, they didn't look up. They didn't wave. They didn't acknowledge the family at all. They walked faster, heads down, like the house itself was dangerous.

Bev's heart cracked a little. Corey felt his stomach drop.

Bobbi Jr clenched his fists. Dee watched silently, his expression unreadable.

Kayla closed her laptop and said the block wasn't turning cold by accident — it was being guided. Red was isolating them. Red was tightening the circle. Red was making sure that when he made his next move, no one would step in. No one would help. No one would speak up.

Aunt Jane whispered that darkness always tried to isolate before it attacked. She said the enemy wanted them alone, wanted them vulnerable, wanted them doubting themselves. Dee nodded slowly, saying Red wasn't getting that victory.

But even as he said it, the truth settled heavy in the room.

The block wasn't just distant. It wasn't just quiet. It wasn't just scared.

The block was choosing survival. And survival meant stepping away from the family. The cold wasn't weather. It was betrayal.

CHAPTER SIXTEEN — Red Makes His Move

The house was still buzzing from the block resident's confession when the first sign of trouble hit. Dee stood in the living room with Kayla, going over the evidence again, trying to piece together Red's timeline, trying to understand how close the danger really was. Corey paced near the window, glancing outside every few seconds, unable to shake the feeling that something was coming. Bev moved through the kitchen with restless energy, wiping down the same counter over and over, her nerves stretched thin. Aunt Jane sat in her chair, eyes half-closed, sensing the shift in the air long before anyone else noticed it.

Bobbi Jr hovered near the hallway, tense, alert, waiting for something he couldn't name. Then the lights flickered. Just once. Quick. Barely noticeable.
But enough to make everyone freeze. Corey stopped pacing. Kayla looked up from her laptop. Bev turned toward the living room. Dee's eyes narrowed. Aunt Jane opened her eyes fully, her voice low as she whispered that the atmosphere had changed. Bobbi Jr stepped forward, asking what that meant, but before anyone could answer, the lights flickered again — longer this time, like the house was holding its breath.

Dee moved toward the window, pulling the curtain back just enough to see the street. The block was quiet, too quiet, the kind of quiet that didn't belong in the 44. No cars. No voices. No movement. Just stillness. Corey stepped beside him, whispering that something felt wrong. Dee didn't respond. He didn't need to. The wrongness was thick enough to taste.
Then, from down the street, a sound echoed — not loud,

not violent, but sharp enough to cut through the silence. A bottle breaking. Bev gasped. Corey stiffened. Kayla closed her laptop slowly. Aunt Jane whispered a prayer under her breath. Bobbi Jr moved closer to the door, his heart pounding.

Dee stepped onto the porch, motioning for Corey to stay behind him. The air outside felt heavy, charged, like the block itself was waiting for something to happen. Dee scanned the street, his eyes sharp, his senses heightened. At first, he didn't see anything. Then he noticed it — a small object sitting in the middle of the road, glinting under the streetlight. A brick. Wrapped in something.

Dee walked down the steps slowly, every instinct on high alert. Corey followed a few steps behind, ignoring Dee's warning look. When they reached the edge of the sidewalk, Dee crouched down, staring at the brick. It was wrapped in a piece of paper, tied with a thin strip of black cloth. A message. A threat. A declaration.

Dee didn't touch it. He didn't need to. He already knew who it was from.
Red.

Corey whispered that they should take it inside, but Dee shook his head, telling him not to touch anything Red left behind. Kayla stepped onto the porch, asking what it was. Dee didn't answer. He just stared at the brick, his jaw tightening, his breath steadying, his mind already calculating the next move.
Aunt Jane stepped into the doorway, her voice soft but strong as she said Red had crossed a line. Bev moved beside her, her hand covering her mouth, fear and anger mixing in

her eyes. Bobbi Jr stood behind them, fists clenched, his chest rising and falling with heavy breaths.

Dee finally spoke, his voice low and steady, saying Red wasn't sending warnings anymore. He was sending promises. Corey swallowed hard, asking what they were supposed to do now. Dee stood up slowly, his expression shifting into something cold, focused, unshakeable. He said they were going to tighten up, stay alert, and prepare — because Red wasn't circling anymore.

He was advancing. And the family needed to be ready. Inside the house, the lights flickered one more time — not from a power issue, but from the weight of the moment settling over the 44.

The war had officially begun.

CHAPTER SEVENTEEN — Tightening the House

The house moved differently the next morning. Nobody said it out loud, but everyone felt it — the shift, the urgency, the sense that Red's message wasn't just a threat but a countdown. Dee woke up before the sun, pacing the living room with a quiet intensity that made the walls feel smaller. He checked the locks twice, then checked them again. He walked the perimeter of the house, scanning every window, every shadow, every corner like he expected something to jump out. Corey watched him from the hallway, feeling the tension in his chest rise with every step Dee took.

Bev moved through the kitchen with a determination that came from fear and love mixed together. She packed a bag of essentials — not because she planned to leave, but because she refused to be caught unprepared. She whispered to herself that she wasn't letting Red take anything from her family. Aunt Jane sat at the table, her hands folded, her eyes closed, whispering prayers that wrapped around the house like invisible armor. She didn't need to see the danger to feel it. She could sense it in the air, thick and heavy, pressing against the walls.

Kayla sat at the dining table with her laptop open, her fingers flying across the keys as she pulled up maps, phone logs, and financial trails. She told Dee that Red wasn't moving randomly — he was moving with intention, precision, strategy. She said the brick wasn't just a warning; it was a marker. A signal. A declaration that the next move would be physical. Dee nodded, his jaw tightening, saying he already knew. He could feel it in his bones.

Bobbi Jr walked into the room, his shoulders tense, his

eyes tired but focused. He said he wanted to help, wanted to do something, wanted to be part of the preparation instead of sitting in the background drowning in guilt. Dee looked at him for a long moment, then nodded, telling him to stay close, stay alert, stay ready. Corey stepped beside him, saying he wasn't letting Bobbi Jr face anything alone. Aunt Jane smiled softly, saying unity was their strength, and Red knew it — that's why he was trying to break it.

The family gathered in the living room, forming a loose circle. Dee laid out the plan — no one went anywhere alone, no one opened the door without checking, no one ignored anything that felt off. He said Red wasn't just testing them anymore; he was advancing. And the family needed to move like a unit. Bev nodded, saying she didn't care what the block thought — she cared about keeping her family alive. Kayla added that the snitch was still out there, still feeding Red information, still helping him tighten the circle. Corey muttered that he wanted to confront them, but Dee shook his head, saying they needed strategy, not impulse.

Just then, a sound echoed outside — not loud, not violent, but sharp enough to make everyone freeze. A car door closing. Slow. Intentional. Dee moved to the window, pulling the curtain back just enough to see. A car sat across the street — not Red's, but one of his people. The engine was off. The windows were tinted. The presence was unmistakable. Corey stepped beside him, whispering that they were being watched again. Dee didn't respond. He didn't need to. The truth was sitting right there in the street.

Aunt Jane stood slowly, her voice steady as she said the enemy was close, closer than they realized. Bev grabbed

Corey's arm, pulling him back from the window. Bobbi Jr clenched his fists, his breath quickening. Kayla closed her laptop, her expression shifting into something sharp and focused.

Dee stepped away from the window, his voice low and calm as he said, "Everybody tighten up. This ain't a warning anymore." The room fell silent. The car didn't move. The block didn't breathe. The house didn't blink. Red wasn't circling. He was watching. Waiting. Measuring. And the family knew — the next move wouldn't be subtle.

CHAPTER EIGHTEEN — The Block Shifts Again

The day moved slow, heavy, and uneasy, like the 44 itself was dragging its feet through something thick and unseen. Dee sat at the dining table with Kayla, both of them staring at the laptop screen without speaking. The evidence was clear, the timeline was clear, the threat was clear — but the next move wasn't. Corey stood near the window, arms crossed, watching the same car that had been parked across the street for over an hour. It didn't move. It didn't blink. It just sat there like a shadow with an engine. Bev walked back and forth between the kitchen and the living room, her nerves stretched thin, her spirit restless. Aunt Jane sat in her chair, eyes half-closed, whispering prayers that felt heavier than usual. Bobbi Jr paced the hallway, unable to sit still, unable to shake the feeling that something was coming.

Then the block shifted again.

It started with a door slamming down the street — loud, sharp, echoing through the quiet like a warning shot. Corey flinched, stepping back from the window. Dee stood up immediately, his instincts kicking in. Bev froze mid-step, her breath catching. Kayla closed her laptop slowly, her expression sharpening. Aunt Jane lifted her head, sensing the change before anyone else could name it. Bobbi Jr stepped into the living room, his eyes wide, his chest rising and falling with quick breaths.

A group of men walked down the block — not Red's people, but people who used to be neutral, people who used to mind their business, people who used to nod at Dee when they passed. Today, they didn't nod. They didn't look at the house. They didn't acknowledge the family at all. They walked with purpose, with tension, with something that felt like fear disguised as loyalty. Corey whispered that the block was choosing sides again. Dee didn't respond. He didn't need to. The truth was walking right in front of them.

Bev stepped closer to the window, her voice trembling as she said she didn't recognize the block anymore. Aunt Jane told her softly that fear made people forget themselves. Kayla added that Red was manipulating the neighborhood — using intimidation, using whispers, using the snitch to twist the narrative. She said the block wasn't turning on the family because they wanted to — they were turning because they were scared. Dee clenched his jaw, saying fear didn't excuse betrayal. Aunt Jane nodded, saying it didn't excuse it, but it explained it.

Just then, the car across the street finally moved — not fast, not aggressive, but slow and deliberate, rolling down the block like it was surveying territory. Corey watched it with a tight chest, whispering that it felt like the car was waiting for something. Dee stepped beside him, his voice low as he said the car wasn't waiting — it was signaling. Bobbi Jr swallowed hard, asking what that meant. Kayla answered before Dee could — she said Red was coordinating something. Something bigger. Something close.

The block grew quieter. The air grew heavier. The tension grew sharper.
Aunt Jane stood slowly, leaning on her cane, her voice steady as she said the enemy was moving in the open now. She said Red wasn't hiding his presence anymore because he didn't have to. He had the block watching for him. He had the snitch feeding him information. He had fear doing half the work.

Bev whispered that she felt sick. Corey whispered that he felt watched. Bobbi Jr whispered that he felt responsible. Kayla whispered that she felt ready. Dee didn't whisper anything. He stood in the center of the room, his expression hardening into something cold and unshakeable.

He said Red wasn't circling anymore. He wasn't warning anymore. He wasn't testing anymore. He was positioning. And the family needed to be ready — because whatever Red was planning next wasn't going to be subtle, quiet, or distant. It was going to be close. Personal. Direct.

The block wasn't shifting by accident. It was shifting because Red was pulling the strings. And the family could feel the tension tightening like a rope around the 44.

CHAPTER NINETEEN — The Snitch Slips Up

The house was tense, the kind of tense that made every sound feel louder than it should. Dee sat at the dining table with Kayla, both of them staring at the laptop screen like it held the key to everything. Corey stood near the window again, watching the street with a sharpness he didn't have a week ago. Bev moved quietly through the kitchen, her nerves stretched thin but her spirit steady. Aunt Jane sat in her chair, eyes half-closed, whispering prayers that wrapped around the house like a shield. Bobbi Jr paced the hallway, restless, alert, waiting for something he couldn't name.

Then Kayla froze.

Her fingers hovered over the keyboard, her eyes narrowing as she leaned closer to the screen. Dee noticed immediately, stepping behind her, asking what she saw. Kayla didn't answer at first. She clicked something, then clicked again, her breath catching as the data lined up in a way it hadn't before. She whispered that the snitch had slipped — finally, unmistakably, publicly.

The room shifted. Corey stepped away from the window. Bev stopped moving. Bobbi Jr came into the living room. Aunt Jane opened her eyes fully, sensing the change in the air.

Kayla turned the laptop toward Dee and pointed at the screen. She explained that the snitch had made a transfer — a sloppy one, rushed, unplanned. It wasn't big, but it was enough to expose a pattern she hadn't seen before. A pattern that connected the snitch's movements to Red's car sightings. A pattern that tied the snitch to the brick left in the street. A pattern that proved the snitch wasn't just talking — they were coordinating.

Dee stared at the screen, his jaw tightening as the truth settled in. Corey whispered that he knew something felt off. Bev shook her head, saying she couldn't believe someone from the block would do this. Bobbi Jr cursed under his breath, pacing again, his anger rising. Aunt Jane leaned forward, her voice steady as she said the truth always revealed itself when darkness got too bold.

Kayla kept talking, her voice sharp and focused. She said the snitch had been near the house earlier than they realized. She said the snitch had been watching the family long before Red made his first move. She said the snitch wasn't acting alone — they were being directed. And now, because of one rushed transfer, she had the exact location the snitch had been at the moment the brick was dropped.

A house. On the block. Too close. Far too close.
Dee stood up slowly, his expression shifting into something cold and controlled. He said the snitch wasn't just feeding Red information — they were helping him plan. Helping him position. Helping him tighten the noose around the family.

Corey asked what they were going to do. Bev whispered that she didn't want violence. Bobbi Jr said he didn't want to sit back anymore. Aunt Jane said they needed wisdom, not rage. Kayla said they needed strategy.

Dee nodded, saying they weren't going to confront the snitch blindly. They were going to watch. They were going to move smart. They were going to protect the house first. Then they would deal with the snitch.

Just then, a shadow moved across the porch — quick, silent, intentional.

Corey stiffened. Bev gasped. Bobbi Jr stepped forward. Kayla closed the laptop. Aunt Jane whispered a prayer. Dee moved toward the door.

The shadow paused. Then disappeared.

The snitch wasn't hiding anymore. They were circling. Watching. Waiting.

And the family knew — the next move was coming soon.

CHAPTER TWENTY — Pressure on the Snitch

The house felt like it was holding its breath. Every room carried tension, every shadow felt heavier, every sound made someone look up. Dee stood in the living room with his arms crossed, staring at the front door like he expected it to open on its own. Corey sat on the edge of the couch, bouncing his knee, unable to sit still. Bev moved quietly through the kitchen, her spirit restless, her nerves stretched thin. Aunt Jane sat in her chair, eyes half-closed, whispering prayers that wrapped around the house like armor. Kayla was at the dining table, her laptop open, her expression sharp. Bobbi Jr leaned against the wall, arms folded, trying to steady his breathing.

Then Kayla's phone buzzed.
She looked down, and her entire expression changed — not fear, not shock, but recognition. She stood up slowly, telling Dee she had just received a notification from one of the monitoring systems she set up. The snitch had made another move. A sloppy one. A rushed one. A panicked one. Dee stepped closer, asking what happened. Kayla said the snitch had just pinged a location — not far, not hidden, not subtle. A house on the block. A house too close for comfort.

Corey stood up immediately, asking if the snitch was there right now. Kayla nodded, saying the snitch had been there for at least twenty minutes. Bev whispered that she knew something felt off earlier. Aunt Jane lifted her head, saying the enemy always got reckless when pressure closed in. Bobbi Jr clenched his fists, whispering that he wanted to go confront them. Dee shook his head, telling him no — not yet. Not without a plan.

Kayla explained that the snitch wasn't just hiding — they were meeting someone. Someone who had pulled up to the house earlier. Someone who didn't belong on the block. Someone who moved like they were delivering instructions. Corey swallowed hard, asking if it was Red. Kayla shook her head, saying it wasn't Red — but it was one of his people. Someone high enough in his circle to carry messages. Someone trusted.

The room shifted. Bev stepped closer to Dee, her voice trembling as she said the snitch was getting bold. Aunt Jane said boldness was a sign of desperation. Bobbi Jr said he didn't care what it was — he wanted answers. Corey nodded, saying they couldn't keep letting the snitch move freely. Kayla agreed, saying the snitch was escalating. She said the snitch wasn't just feeding Red information anymore — they were helping him plan the next move.

Dee finally spoke, his voice low and steady. He said they weren't going to confront the snitch tonight — not without knowing what Red's people were doing. He said they needed to watch, to observe, to gather information. He said the snitch wasn't the only threat — the person they were meeting was just as dangerous. Maybe more.

Just then, headlights flashed outside — once, twice, slow and deliberate. Corey stiffened. Bev gasped. Kayla closed her laptop. Bobbi Jr stepped forward. Aunt Jane whispered a prayer. Dee moved toward the window.

A car rolled down the block — not fast, not loud, but intentional. It slowed near the house where the snitch was hiding. The passenger window slid down just enough for a hand to appear — a gloved hand — tapping twice on the door frame before the car pulled off.

A signal. A message. A command.
Kayla whispered that she recognized the pattern — it was the same timing as the brick. The same timing as the bullet. The same timing as the surveillance car.

Red wasn't circling. He wasn't watching. He wasn't waiting.
He was coordinating.
And the snitch was following orders.

Dee stepped back from the window, his expression hardening into something cold and unshakeable. He said the family needed to tighten up even more. He said the snitch wasn't acting alone. He said Red was moving pieces on the board.

And the next move was coming soon.
The house fell silent. The block held its breath. The night grew heavier.
The pressure wasn't just on the family now. It was on the snitch too.
And pressure made people crack.

CHAPTER TWENTY-ONE — Cracks in the Snitch

The snitch didn't sleep that night. Not really. They paced their small living room, checking the blinds every few minutes, jumping at every car that passed, every dog that barked, every shadow that moved. Red's people had come by earlier — not to threaten, not to reassure, but to remind. Remind them of the deal. Remind them of the consequences. Remind them that once you started talking, you didn't get to stop. The snitch's hands shook as they replayed the meeting in their mind, the gloved hand tapping twice on the doorframe, the silent message that said everything without saying a word.

Across the block, the family was awake too. Dee stood in the living room, staring at the front door like he could feel the snitch's fear from across the street. Corey sat on the couch, bouncing his knee, whispering that something felt off. Bev moved through the kitchen with restless energy, unable to settle. Aunt Jane sat in her chair, eyes half-closed, whispering prayers that wrapped around the house like a shield. Kayla was at the dining table, her laptop open, tracking the snitch's movements with a precision that made the room feel smaller. Bobbi Jr leaned against the wall, arms folded, his breath steady but his spirit restless.

Then Kayla's screen lit up.

A new ping. A new location. A new mistake.

She stood up quickly, telling Dee the snitch had moved again — not far, but fast, like they were running from something. Dee asked where. Kayla pointed to the map, her voice sharp as she said the snitch was heading toward the back of the block, near the alley behind the old corner store.

Corey stiffened, saying nobody went back there unless they were hiding. Bev whispered that she felt sick. Aunt Jane lifted her head, saying the enemy was stirring. Bobbi Jr stepped forward, asking if they were going after the snitch now.

Dee shook his head, saying they weren't moving blind. He said they needed to watch first, understand the pattern, understand the fear. Kayla nodded, saying the snitch wasn't acting bold anymore — they were acting scared. She said the snitch wasn't moving like someone loyal to Red. They were moving like someone trapped between two fires.

The snitch reached the alley, breathing hard, looking over their shoulder every few seconds. They pulled out their phone, typing fast, deleting, typing again, deleting again. They didn't know who to call. Red? No — Red didn't tolerate weakness. The family? No — the family didn't tolerate betrayal. They were stuck in the middle, drowning in the consequences of their own choices.

A car rolled slowly into the alley — not Red's, but one of his people. The snitch froze, their breath catching in their chest. The passenger window slid down just enough for a voice to speak — low, calm, dangerous. The voice told them they were slipping. The voice told them Red didn't like mistakes. The voice told them pressure made people talk too much.

The snitch swallowed hard, nodding quickly, promising they were still loyal, still committed, still useful. The voice didn't respond. The window slid up. The car pulled off.

The snitch stood alone in the alley, shaking.

Across the block, Kayla watched the movement on her screen, her expression tightening. She told Dee the snitch wasn't just scared — they were cracking. Corey whispered that cracks made people dangerous. Bev said cracks made people unpredictable. Aunt Jane said cracks made people reveal themselves. Bobbi Jr said cracks made people desperate.

Dee nodded slowly, saying the snitch was reaching their breaking point. And when people broke, they made mistakes. Big ones. Loud ones. Deadly ones.

The family didn't know when the snitch would crack But they knew it was coming. And when it did, the whole block would feel it.

CHAPTER TWENTY-TWO — Desperation on the Block

The snitch didn't go home after the alley meeting. They couldn't. Their nerves were shot, their hands shaking, their breath uneven. Instead, they wandered the block like a ghost, sticking to shadows, avoiding streetlights, jumping at every sound. Red's people had made it clear — mistakes wouldn't be tolerated. And the snitch had made too many already. They felt the pressure closing in from both sides, squeezing their chest until it hurt to breathe.

Across the block, the family felt the shift too. Dee stood in the living room, staring at the front door like he could sense the snitch's panic from across the street. Corey sat on the couch, bouncing his knee, whispering that something felt wrong. Bev moved through the kitchen with restless energy, wiping down the same counter over and over. Aunt Jane sat in her chair, eyes half-closed, whispering prayers that wrapped around the house like a shield. Kayla was at the dining table, her laptop open, tracking every movement the snitch made. Bobbi Jr leaned against the wall, arms folded, his breath steady but his spirit restless.

Then Kayla's screen lit up again.
Another ping. Another location. Another mistake.
She stood up quickly, telling Dee the snitch had doubled back — not toward home, not toward Red's people, but toward the abandoned duplex near the end of the block. Corey stiffened, saying nobody went near that place unless they were hiding. Bev whispered that she felt sick. Aunt Jane lifted her head, saying the enemy was stirring again. Bobbi Jr stepped forward, asking if this was it — if the snitch was finally breaking.

Kayla nodded slowly, saying the snitch wasn't moving with purpose anymore. They were moving with fear. She said the snitch wasn't acting like someone loyal to Red — they were acting like someone trying to escape him. Dee clenched his jaw, saying fear made people dangerous. Corey added that fear made people sloppy. Aunt Jane said fear made people reveal themselves. Bobbi Jr said fear made people desperate.

The snitch reached the duplex, breathing hard, looking over their shoulder every few seconds. They slipped inside through a broken side door, their footsteps echoing in the empty space. They pulled out their phone, typing fast, deleting, typing again, deleting again. They didn't know who to call. Red? No — Red didn't tolerate weakness. The family? No — the family didn't tolerate betrayal. They were trapped between two storms, and both were closing in.

Inside the duplex, the snitch paced the dusty floor, whispering to themselves, trying to figure out how everything had gone so wrong. They replayed every message they sent Red, every detail they shared, every moment they thought they were safe. They weren't safe now. They weren't protected. They weren't valued. They were disposable.

A car rolled slowly past the duplex — not Red's, but one of his people. The snitch froze, their breath catching in their chest. The car didn't stop. It didn't speed up. It just crawled past, slow and deliberate, like it was reminding them that escape wasn't an option.

Across the block, Kayla watched the movement on her screen, her expression tightening. She told Dee the snitch was spiraling. Corey whispered that spiraling people made mistakes. Bev said spiraling people made noise. Aunt Jane said spiraling people revealed truth. Bobbi Jr said spiraling people were dangerous.

Dee nodded slowly, saying the snitch was reaching their breaking point.
And when people broke, they didn't break quietly.
Just then, the snitch's phone buzzed — a message from an unknown number.

They stared at it, their hands shaking, their breath uneven.

The message was short. Cold. Final.

"You're slipping. Fix it."

The snitch dropped the phone, their knees buckling as the weight of the threat hit them full force.

Across the block, the family felt the shift — the moment fear turned into desperation.
The snitch wasn't hiding anymore. They were unraveling.
And unraveling people were unpredictable.

CHAPTER TWENTY-THREE — The Snitch Starts to Unravel

The sun hadn't even fully risen when the block felt... off. Not tense, not quiet — off. The kind of off that made people peek through blinds and step onto porches with folded arms and narrowed eyes. Dee felt it the moment he opened the front door. The air was heavy, thick, unsettled. Corey stepped beside him, whispering that something didn't feel right. Dee didn't respond. He didn't need to. The truth was sitting in the middle of the street.

The snitch.
They weren't hiding anymore. They weren't sneaking. They weren't blending in. They were unraveling. The snitch stood near the corner, pacing back and forth, talking to themselves, their hands shaking, their movements jerky and frantic. People on the block watched from a distance — not helping, not approaching, just watching. Fear made people curious. Fear made people quiet. Fear made people step back.

Bev stepped onto the porch, her hand covering her mouth as she whispered that she had never seen the snitch look like that. Aunt Jane moved behind her, leaning on her cane, her voice soft but steady as she said the enemy was tightening the rope. Kayla came to the doorway, her laptop still in her hand, saying the snitch had been pinging random locations all morning — no pattern, no purpose, just panic. Bobbi Jr stepped outside too, his chest rising and falling with heavy breaths, watching the snitch like he expected them to collapse.

Then it happened. The snitch stopped pacing. Stopped

talking.

Stopped breathing for a moment. They turned toward the family's house.

Not with confidence. Not with anger. With fear. Pure, raw fear.

They took a step forward, then another, their eyes wide, their breath uneven. Corey whispered that they were coming toward the house. Bev grabbed his arm, pulling him back. Kayla stepped forward, her expression sharp. Aunt Jane whispered a prayer under her breath. Bobbi Jr clenched his fists. Dee stepped off the porch, meeting the snitch halfway down the sidewalk.

The snitch froze when they saw him. Their lips trembled. Their eyes darted around like they were expecting Red's people to appear out of thin air. Dee didn't say anything. He just stood there, calm, steady, unshaken.

The snitch swallowed hard, their voice cracking as they said they needed help. They said they didn't know what to do. They said Red was watching them. They said Red didn't trust them anymore. They said Red thought they were slipping. They said Red sent someone to "check on them" last night. They said they didn't sleep. They said they couldn't breathe. They said they were scared.

Dee didn't move. Didn't blink. Didn't soften.

He asked one question — not loud, not aggressive, just steady. "Why'd you do it?" The snitch broke. They dropped to their knees right there on the sidewalk, crying, shaking, whispering that they didn't mean for it to go this far. They said they were scared of Red. They said Red promised protection. They said Red threatened their family. They said they didn't think it would get this bad. They said they didn't know Red would escalate. They said they didn't know the family would be targeted. They said they didn't know how to stop it.

Bev stepped forward, tears in her eyes, whispering that betrayal always came with excuses. Corey looked away, unable to watch. Bobbi Jr clenched his jaw, anger and pity fighting inside him. Kayla watched with cold clarity, seeing the truth in every word and every lie. Aunt Jane stepped closer, her voice soft but firm as she said the snitch wasn't crying because they were sorry — they were crying because they were caught.

The snitch looked up at Dee, begging him to help, begging him to protect them, begging him to save them from Red.

Dee didn't answer.

Because before he could, a car turned the corner — slow, deliberate, familiar. Red's people. The snitch's eyes widened in terror. The family stiffened. The block held its breath.

And Dee realized something in that moment — the snitch wasn't the only one unraveling.
The whole block was.

CHAPTER TWENTY-FOUR — Red's Shadow on the Street

The car turned the corner slow, deliberate, like it had all the time in the world. Dee didn't move. He stood in the middle of the sidewalk with the snitch kneeling at his feet, tears streaking down their face, their breath coming in short, panicked bursts. Corey stepped closer to the porch, his body tense, ready to move if Dee needed him. Bev grabbed the railing, whispering a prayer under her breath. Kayla stood in the doorway, her laptop still in her hand, her eyes sharp and unblinking. Aunt Jane leaned forward in her chair, her voice soft as she whispered another layer of protection over the family. Bobbi Jr stood beside the steps, fists clenched, jaw tight, watching everything with a storm brewing behind his eyes.

The car didn't speed up. Didn't slow down. Didn't swerve. It just crawled down the block like a shadow with wheels. The snitch looked up, their eyes wide with terror, whispering that Red's people were coming for them. Dee didn't look down. He kept his eyes on the car, his expression unreadable, his stance steady. The snitch grabbed his pant leg, begging him to help, begging him to protect them, begging him not to let Red take them. Dee didn't move. Didn't speak. Didn't promise anything. Because promises were dangerous now.

The car rolled to a stop halfway down the block — not in front of the family's house, not in front of the snitch, but close enough to make its presence felt. The passenger window slid down just an inch, just enough for a pair of eyes to appear. Cold eyes. Calculating eyes. Eyes that didn't blink.

Corey whispered that it wasn't Red — but it was someone close. Bev stepped back, her hand covering her mouth. Kayla narrowed her eyes, recognizing the pattern, the timing, the message. Aunt Jane whispered that darkness didn't always show its face — sometimes it sent shadows. Bobbi Jr took a step forward, but Dee lifted a hand slightly, stopping him without looking away from the car.

The snitch started shaking harder, whispering that they didn't mean to betray anyone, that they didn't want this, that they didn't know how to fix it. Dee finally spoke, his voice low and steady, asking them one question — not why they did it, but who else knew. The snitch swallowed hard, their voice cracking as they said Red had more than one person watching the block. More than one person feeding him information. More than one person waiting for orders.

The family froze. Kayla stepped forward, her voice sharp as she asked how many. The snitch shook their head, saying they didn't know — they only knew Red had a "circle," and they weren't the only one in it. Corey whispered that the block was deeper in Red's pocket than they realized. Bev whispered that she felt sick. Aunt Jane whispered that truth was finally showing its full face. Bobbi Jr whispered that they needed to move now.

    The car's engine revved — low, controlled, intentional.
    The snitch flinched so hard they nearly fell over.
    Dee didn't move.

The car rolled forward a few feet, then stopped again. The passenger window slid down another inch. A hand appeared — gloved, steady, familiar. It tapped twice on the doorframe.

The same signal from the alley. The same signal from the brick. The same signal from the bullet.

Kayla whispered that it was a command. A warning. A countdown.

The snitch broke completely, collapsing onto the sidewalk, sobbing, begging

Dee not to let them die. Corey stepped forward, torn between anger and pity. Bev cried quietly. Aunt Jane whispered a prayer that felt like a shield. Bobbi Jr took another step, ready to move, ready to protect, ready to fight.

The car didn't wait for a response.

It pulled off slow, turning the corner without a sound, leaving the block colder than it found it.

Dee finally looked down at the snitch, his voice low and steady as he said, "Get up."

Because Red wasn't circling anymore. He wasn't watching. He wasn't waiting.

He was here.

And the family had no choice but to face him.

CHAPTER TWENTY-FIVE — Inside the House

Dee didn't say another word. He just looked down at the snitch — broken, shaking, terrified — and told them to get up. His voice wasn't loud, but it carried enough weight to make the snitch scramble to their feet, wiping their face with trembling hands. Corey stepped back to give them space, but his eyes never left them. Bev moved aside, her arms crossed tight, her spirit torn between anger and disbelief. Kayla stood in the doorway, her expression sharp, already analyzing every detail. Aunt Jane watched from her chair, her presence steady, her prayers wrapping around the room like a shield. Bobbi Jr stood near the steps, his jaw tight, his fists clenched, his breath heavy.

Dee walked the snitch toward the house, slow and controlled, like he was escorting a dangerous animal that might bolt at any moment. The snitch kept glancing over their shoulder, terrified Red's people would come back around the corner. They whispered that they didn't want to die. Dee didn't respond. He opened the door and motioned them inside.

The moment the snitch stepped into the living room, the air shifted. The house felt smaller, tighter, heavier. The snitch stood in the center of the room, looking around like they expected judgment to fall from the ceiling. Corey leaned against the wall, arms crossed, eyes sharp. Bev stood near the kitchen, her face tight with hurt. Kayla sat at the dining table, her laptop open, ready to catch every lie. Aunt Jane watched quietly, her spirit reading deeper than words. Bobbi Jr paced behind the couch, unable to stand still.

Dee closed the door and locked it.
Then he turned to the snitch.
"Talk."

The snitch swallowed hard, their voice shaking as they said they didn't mean for any of this to happen. They said Red approached them months ago. They said he offered protection. They said he threatened their family. They said they didn't think it would get this far. They said they didn't know Red would escalate. They said they didn't know the family would be targeted. They said they didn't know how to stop it.

Kayla cut in, her voice sharp as she asked how long they'd been feeding Red information. The snitch hesitated, then whispered the truth — longer than anyone realized. Corey cursed under his breath. Bev shook her head, tears forming. Aunt Jane whispered that betrayal always grew in silence. Bobbi Jr stopped pacing, staring at the snitch with a storm behind his eyes.

Dee stepped closer, asking what Red wanted now. The snitch's voice cracked as they said Red wanted control — of the block, of the narrative, of the fear. They said Red didn't trust them anymore. They said Red thought they were slipping. They said Red sent someone to "check on them" last night. They said they were scared Red would kill them for messing up.

Kayla leaned forward, asking if Red had more people on the block. The snitch nodded quickly, saying Red had a circle — people who watched, people who listened, people who blended in. People the family didn't even suspect.

Corey stiffened. Bev gasped. Aunt Jane whispered that darkness always hid in familiar faces. Bobbi Jr muttered that the block was deeper in Red's pocket than they thought.

The snitch kept talking, their words spilling out faster now, like a dam breaking. They said Red was planning something. Something big. Something close. Something meant to send a message. Dee's jaw tightened. Kayla's fingers flew across her keyboard. Corey stepped closer. Bev covered her mouth. Aunt Jane whispered another prayer. Bobbi Jr clenched his fists.

Then the snitch said something that made the room freeze.
They said Red wasn't just targeting the family.
He was targeting someone specific.
Someone inside the house.
The room went silent.

Dee stepped forward, his voice low and steady as he asked who.
The snitch opened their mouth — but before they could answer, a loud thud hit the side of the house.
Everyone jumped. Corey ran to the window. Bev gasped. Kayla snapped her laptop shut. Aunt Jane whispered a prayer. Bobbi Jr moved toward the door.

Dee raised a hand, stopping everyone.
The snitch backed into the corner, shaking violently.
Red wasn't circling anymore. He wasn't watching. He wasn't waiting.
He was knocking.

CHAPTER TWENTY-SIX — The House Holds Its Breath

The thud against the side of the house echoed through the living room like a warning shot. Not loud enough to break anything, not soft enough to ignore — intentional. Deliberate. A message. Dee didn't flinch. He stood in the center of the room, his eyes locked on the front door, his body still as stone. Corey moved toward the window, but Dee lifted a hand, stopping him without speaking. Bev gasped, her hand flying to her chest as she backed toward the kitchen. Kayla snapped her laptop shut, her eyes sharp and calculating. Aunt Jane whispered a prayer under her breath, her voice steady even as the air thickened. Bobbi Jr stepped closer to the door, his fists clenched, his breath heavy.

The snitch pressed themselves into the corner, shaking violently, whispering that Red had found them. That Red was coming. That Red didn't miss. Dee didn't look at them. He didn't need to. The fear rolling off the snitch was loud enough to fill the room.

Another sound followed — not a thud this time, but footsteps. Slow. Heavy. Purposeful. Moving along the side of the house like someone was tracing the walls with their presence. Corey swallowed hard, whispering that someone was outside. Bev whispered that she felt sick. Kayla whispered that the timing matched the pattern. Aunt Jane whispered that darkness was walking the perimeter. Bobbi Jr whispered that he was ready.

Dee didn't whisper anything.
He stepped toward the door, his movements controlled,

his expression unreadable. He didn't open it. He didn't call out. He just stood there, listening. The footsteps paused. The silence stretched. The house held its breath.

Then a voice — low, muffled, but unmistakably intentional — spoke from outside.

Not a threat. Not a shout. A message.
Short. Cold. Calculated.
The snitch collapsed to the floor, sobbing, covering their ears as if the words themselves were knives. Corey stiffened. Bev cried out softly. Kayla's eyes widened. Aunt Jane whispered another prayer. Bobbi Jr took a step forward, ready to move, ready to protect, ready to fight.

Dee didn't move.

He waited until the footsteps faded, until the presence outside drifted away, until the block fell silent again. Only then did he turn back to the family.

Kayla opened her laptop again, her fingers flying across the keys as she tried to match the timing, the sound, the direction. She said the voice wasn't random — it was coordinated. She said Red wasn't sending people to scare them. He was sending people to test the house. To measure reactions. To see who panicked. To see who stayed calm. To see who cracked.

The snitch lifted their head, tears streaming down their face, whispering that Red was done playing. They said Red didn't trust them anymore. They said Red thought they were slipping. They said Red sent someone to deliver a final warning. Dee stepped closer, his voice low and steady as he asked again, "Who is he targeting?" The snitch hesitated — not because they didn't know, but because saying it out loud made it real. Made it dangerous. Made it irreversible.

They whispered the answer. And the room froze.

Bev covered her mouth. Corey's eyes widened. Kayla's fingers stopped moving. Aunt Jane closed her eyes. Bobbi Jr cursed under his breath. Dee's jaw tightened. Because the target wasn't random. Wasn't weak. Wasn't unprotected.

Red was aiming for someone who mattered. Someone who would break the family if they fell. Someone whose absence would echo through the 44.

The snitch whispered the name again, softer this time, like the walls themselves might carry it back to Red.

And Dee realized something in that moment — Red wasn't trying to scare them. He was trying to destabilize them. And he had just chosen the perfect pressure point.

CHAPTER TWENTY-SEVEN — The Target Revealed

The name hung in the air like smoke — heavy, choking, impossible to ignore. The snitch whispered it again, softer this time, as if saying it too loud would summon Red himself. Dee didn't move. He stood in the center of the living room, his jaw tight, his eyes dark, his breath steady. Corey froze near the window, his chest rising and falling in sharp bursts. Bev covered her mouth, tears forming instantly. Kayla's fingers hovered above her keyboard, suspended in disbelief. Aunt Jane closed her eyes, whispering a prayer that felt heavier than any she'd spoken before. Bobbi Jr stepped forward, his entire body tensing, his fists clenching so hard his knuckles turned white.

Red wasn't targeting the weakest. He wasn't targeting the easiest. He wasn't targeting the most exposed. He was targeting the heart. The snitch kept talking, their voice shaking as they explained that Red didn't want chaos — he wanted collapse. He wanted the family broken from the inside. He wanted the block to see the family fall. He wanted to send a message that would echo through the 44. Corey whispered that Red was playing chess, not checkers. Bev whispered that she felt sick. Kayla whispered that the pattern made sense now. Aunt Jane whispered that the enemy always aimed for the foundation. Bobbi Jr whispered that Red had crossed a line.

Dee finally spoke, his voice low and steady, asking the snitch how long Red had been planning this. The snitch swallowed hard, saying weeks — maybe months. They said Red had been watching, waiting, studying. They said Red knew exactly who to hit to cause the most damage. They said Red didn't want a fight. He wanted a collapse. Kayla stepped forward, her voice sharp as she asked if Red had already made a move. The snitch nodded slowly, saying the thud on the house wasn't random. It wasn't a warning. It was a signal — a message to the circle that the plan had started. Corey stiffened. Bev cried quietly. Aunt Jane whispered another prayer. Bobbi Jr cursed under his breath.

Dee didn't react. Not outwardly. But something shifted in him — something cold, something focused, something unshakeable. He asked the snitch what Red expected them to do next. The snitch whispered that Red wanted panic. He wanted fear. He wanted the family to scatter. He wanted them to make mistakes. He wanted them to turn on each other. He wanted them vulnerable.

Kayla shook her head, saying Red underestimated them. Corey nodded, saying they weren't breaking. Bev wiped her tears, saying they weren't running. Aunt Jane lifted her chin, saying they weren't alone. Bobbi Jr stepped closer to Dee, saying they were ready. The snitch looked around the room, their voice cracking as they said Red didn't care about them anymore. They said Red thought they were slipping. They said Red sent someone to "check on them" earlier. They said they didn't know how much time they had left.

Then — another sound outside. Not a thud. Not footsteps. A car door closing. Slow. Heavy. Intentional. Corey moved toward the window. Bev grabbed his arm. Kayla stood up. Aunt Jane whispered a prayer. Bobbi Jr stepped forward. The snitch collapsed to the floor again. Dee lifted a hand, stopping everyone.

The block fell silent. The air thickened. The danger

pressed against the walls.

Red wasn't circling. He wasn't watching. He wasn't waiting. He was positioning. And the family knew — the next chapter wouldn't be quiet.

CHAPTER TWENTY-EIGHT — Pressure in the Walls

The house felt smaller after the thud. Not physically — spiritually. The air was thick, heavy, almost humming with tension. Dee stood in the center of the living room, his body still, his mind moving fast. Corey hovered near the window, trying to see through the darkness without giving away their position. Bev stood in the kitchen doorway, her hands trembling even as she tried to hide it. Kayla sat at the dining table, her laptop open but untouched, her eyes locked on the snitch. Aunt Jane whispered prayers under her breath, each one layering over the house like invisible armor. Bobbi Jr paced behind the couch, his breath sharp, his fists clenched, his spirit restless.

The snitch sat on the floor, knees pulled to their chest, rocking slightly as they whispered that Red wasn't bluffing. They said Red didn't send warnings twice. They said the voice outside wasn't random — it was a message. A countdown. A promise. Dee didn't look at them. He didn't need to. The fear rolling off the snitch was loud enough to fill the room.

Kayla finally broke the silence, her voice low but steady as she said the timing matched Red's pattern. She said the thud, the footsteps, the voice — all of it lined up with the signals she'd been tracking. She said Red wasn't improvising. He was executing. Corey swallowed hard, whispering that the block felt different tonight. Bev nodded, saying she felt it too — like the walls themselves were listening. Aunt Jane lifted her head, saying darkness always pressed hardest right before it broke. Bobbi Jr muttered that he was tired of waiting.

Dee finally spoke, his voice calm but sharp as steel. He said Red wasn't trying to scare them anymore — he was trying to destabilize them. He said Red wanted them rattled. Wanted them divided. Wanted them reacting instead of thinking. Kayla nodded, saying that's why Red chose the target he did. Corey whispered that the target made everything personal. Bev whispered that the target made everything dangerous. Aunt Jane whispered that the target made everything spiritual. Bobbi Jr whispered that the target made everything war.

The snitch lifted their head, tears streaking down their face, whispering that Red didn't trust them anymore. They said Red thought they were slipping. They said Red sent someone to "check on them" earlier. They said they didn't know how much time they had left. Dee stepped closer, asking what Red expected them to do next. The snitch swallowed hard, saying Red wanted them to finish the job — to deliver the final piece of information. The piece that would let Red strike.

Kayla leaned forward, her voice sharp as she asked what that piece was. The snitch hesitated, shaking, whispering that they didn't want to say it. Corey stepped forward, anger rising. Bev whispered that they needed the truth. Aunt Jane whispered that truth was the only weapon they had. Bobbi Jr whispered that the snitch owed them that much.

The snitch finally spoke.
They said Red wanted to know when the family would be separated — even for a moment. When someone would

step outside alone. When someone would go to the store. When someone would take out the trash. When someone would walk to the car. When someone would check the mail.

Red didn't want a shootout. He wanted an opening.
A small one. A quiet one. A perfect one.
Dee's jaw tightened. Kayla's eyes narrowed. Corey's breath caught. Bev covered her mouth. Aunt Jane whispered a prayer. Bobbi Jr cursed under his breath.

The snitch whispered that Red wasn't planning chaos. He was planning precision. Then — another sound outside. Not a thud. Not footsteps. A soft scrape. Like someone dragging something across the siding. Corey stiffened. Bev gasped. Kayla stood up. Aunt Jane whispered faster. Bobbi Jr moved toward the door. Dee raised a hand, stopping everyone.

The scrape stopped. Silence. Then a soft tap — right beneath the living room window. The snitch screamed. And the house realized something at the same time: Red wasn't testing the walls. He was mapping them

CHAPTER TWENTY-NINE — The Walls Start Talking

The tap beneath the window echoed through the living room like a whisper from the dark — soft, intentional, chilling. Dee didn't move. He stood in the center of the room, his body still, his mind calculating. Corey froze near the window, his breath caught in his throat. Bev backed into the kitchen doorway, her hand pressed to her chest. Kayla stood up slowly, her laptop forgotten on the table. Aunt Jane whispered a prayer that wrapped around the room like a shield. Bobbi Jr stepped forward, ready to move, ready to protect, ready to fight.

The snitch curled tighter into the corner, shaking so hard their teeth chattered. They whispered that Red was here. That Red was watching. That Red was marking the house. Dee didn't look at them. He didn't need to. The fear rolling off the snitch was loud enough to fill the room. Another sound followed — a soft scrape along the siding, like someone dragging a finger or a tool across the wall. Slow. Deliberate. Mapping. Corey whispered that they were tracing the house. Bev whispered that she felt sick. Kayla whispered that the pattern matched Red's surveillance style. Aunt Jane whispered that darkness always studied before it struck. Bobbi Jr whispered that he was tired of being hunted.

Dee finally stepped toward the window, but he didn't pull the curtain back. He didn't want to give Red's people the satisfaction of seeing movement. Instead, he listened — really listened — to the rhythm of the scrape. It wasn't random. It wasn't sloppy. It was measured. Calculated. Like someone marking points on a blueprint. Kayla moved closer, her voice low as she said Red wasn't just watching the house — he was learning it. Studying it. Memorizing it. She said the scrape wasn't a threat. It was a map. Corey swallowed hard, whispering that Red was planning something precise. Bev whispered that she didn't want to hear any more. Aunt Jane whispered that truth didn't care about comfort. Bobbi Jr whispered that they needed to act.

The snitch lifted their head, tears streaking down their face, whispering that Red didn't trust them anymore. They said Red thought they were slipping. They said Red sent someone to "check on them" earlier. They said Red wanted to know when the family would be separated — even for a moment. Dee's jaw tightened. Kayla's eyes narrowed. Corey's breath caught. Bev covered her mouth. Aunt Jane whispered another prayer. Bobbi Jr cursed under his breath.

Then — silence. The scrape stopped. The tapping stopped. The footsteps stopped. The block held its breath.

Dee stepped back from the window, his voice low and steady as he said Red wasn't testing the house anymore. He was preparing it. Kayla nodded, saying Red was building a blueprint. Corey whispered that the blueprint wasn't for intimidation. Bev whispered that the blueprint wasn't for fear. Aunt Jane whispered that the blueprint wasn't for show. Bobbi Jr whispered that the blueprint was for attack.

The snitch started crying again, whispering that they didn't want to die. Dee finally turned to them, his voice sharp as he asked what Red's next move was. The snitch hesitated, shaking, whispering that Red didn't tell them everything — only enough to keep them scared. Only enough to keep them useful. Only enough to keep them loyal. Kayla stepped forward, her voice cutting through the room as she asked what Red expected them to deliver next. The snitch swallowed hard, whispering that Red wanted one thing:

A moment of vulnerability.

A door unlocked. A window cracked. A light turned off. A person stepping outside alone. Red didn't want chaos. He wanted precision. Dee nodded slowly, his expression shifting into something cold and unshakeable. He said the family wasn't giving Red anything. Not a moment. Not a window. Not a breath. Then — another sound. A car engine. Slow. Deep. Familiar. Corey stiffened. Bev gasped. Kayla looked up sharply. Aunt Jane whispered faster. Bobbi Jr moved toward the door. The snitch screamed.

Dee raised a hand, stopping everyone. The engine idled outside the house.
Not moving. Not leaving. Waiting. Red wasn't mapping anymore.
He was positioning. And the family knew — Chapter Thirty wouldn't be quiet.

CHAPTER THIRTY — The Weight of What's Coming

The house felt heavier than it had all week, like the walls themselves were holding their breath. Dee stood in the hallway, staring at the front door as if he expected it to speak. Kayla watched him from the dining room table, her laptop open but untouched, her mind racing through every detail she couldn't say out loud. Corey sat on the couch, bouncing his knee, glancing at the window every few seconds, whispering that the block felt wrong tonight. Bev moved slowly through the kitchen, wiping the same counter over and over, her prayers quieter now, more desperate, more like she was bargaining with God.

Aunt Jane sat in her favorite chair, hands folded, eyes closed, whispering strength into the room the way only she could. Bobbi Jr leaned against the wall, arms crossed, jaw tight, ready for whatever storm was inching closer. And the snitch — shaking, sweating, unraveling — kept whispering that Red wasn't done, that he was circling, that he was waiting for the perfect moment to strike.

Dee finally spoke, his voice low, steady, dangerous. He said Red wasn't moving like he used to. He said this wasn't random. He said Red was building something — a plan, a message, a moment — and when it hit, it wouldn't be loud. It would be personal. Kayla swallowed hard, asking what he meant, but Dee didn't answer. He didn't have to. The silence said enough.

Aunt Jane opened her eyes and told them the truth nobody wanted to hear — the bloodline was shifting. Not breaking. Not falling apart. Shifting. She said every family had a moment where the past and the present collided, where the truth demanded to be heard, where the legacy chose who was strong enough to carry it. She said their moment was coming. She said they needed to be ready.

Corey whispered that he'd seen a car earlier, parked too long, lights off, engine running. Kayla asked why he didn't say anything. Corey said he didn't want to scare anyone. Bobbi Jr snapped that fear wasn't the problem — silence was. The snitch started crying, saying Red was watching them, saying Red was closer than they thought, saying Red wasn't coming for him anymore. He was coming for the family.

Dee stepped forward, his voice sharp as he told the snitch to stop talking unless he was ready to tell the whole truth. The snitch froze. The room froze with him. Aunt Jane whispered that truth was the only thing that could save them now. Kayla whispered that lies were killing them faster than Red ever could. Bev whispered that she felt something coming, something heavy, something final.

The snitch finally spoke.
He said Red wasn't working alone. He said someone inside the block was feeding him information. He said someone close — too close — had been moving in the shadows.
The room went silent.

Dee didn't blink. Kayla didn't breathe. Corey's knee stopped bouncing. Bev dropped the rag. Aunt Jane whispered a prayer of protection. Bobbi Jr stepped forward. The snitch trembled harder.

Dee asked for a name.

The snitch opened his mouth.
And the lights flickered.

Once. Twice. Then the whole house went dark.
The block outside fell silent.

And everyone in the room knew — **whatever was coming next was already on its way.**

CHAPTER THIRTY ONE— The Engine in the Dark

The engine outside rumbled low, steady, patient — the kind of idle that wasn't accidental. Dee stood in the center of the living room, his body still, his mind sharp, his senses tuned to every vibration in the walls. Corey hovered near the window, careful not to touch the curtain, his breath shallow. Bev backed into the kitchen doorway, whispering a prayer she didn't even realize she was saying. Kayla stood at the dining table, her laptop open but untouched, her eyes locked on the front door. Aunt Jane whispered softly, her voice steady, her spirit anchoring the room. Bobbi Jr moved closer to Dee, his fists clenched, his jaw tight, his breath heavy.

The snitch curled into the corner, shaking violently, whispering that the engine meant Red was here. That Red was watching. That Red was waiting for the perfect moment. Dee didn't look at them. He didn't need to. The fear rolling off the snitch was loud enough to fill the room. The engine revved once — low, controlled, intentional. Corey stiffened. Bev gasped. Kayla's eyes narrowed. Aunt Jane whispered another layer of protection. Bobbi Jr stepped forward, ready to move. Dee lifted a hand, stopping him.

The engine settled again, humming like a heartbeat in the dark.

Kayla finally spoke, her voice low but steady as she said the timing matched Red's pattern. She said the engine wasn't random. It was a signal. A marker. A presence. Corey whispered that the car wasn't moving because it didn't need to. Bev whispered that she felt like the house was being watched from every angle. Aunt Jane whispered that darkness always announced itself before it struck. Bobbi Jr whispered that he was tired of being hunted.

Dee stepped toward the door, but he didn't open it. He didn't call out. He didn't show fear. He just stood there, listening. The engine idled, steady and unbothered, like whoever sat inside wasn't in a rush. Like they were waiting for something. Or someone.

The snitch lifted their head, tears streaking down their face, whispering that Red wasn't bluffing. They said Red didn't send cars to sit. He sent cars to watch. To measure. To time. Dee finally turned to them, his voice sharp as he asked what Red wanted next. The snitch swallowed hard, whispering that Red wanted vulnerability. A moment. A slip. A crack. Kayla stepped forward, her voice cutting through the room as she said Red wasn't planning chaos — he was planning precision. Corey nodded, whispering that the engine was part of the plan. Bev whispered that she didn't want to hear any more. Aunt Jane whispered that truth didn't care about comfort. Bobbi Jr whispered that they needed to act. Then — the engine revved again. Longer this time

. Deeper. Closer.

Dee stepped back from the door, his expression shifting into something cold and unshakeable. He said Red wasn't circling anymore. He wasn't mapping. He wasn't testing. He was positioning.

Kayla moved to the window, careful not to be seen, her voice low as she said the car hadn't moved an inch. Corey whispered that the block felt like it was holding its breath. Bev whispered that she felt like something was about to break. Aunt Jane whispered that the storm had reached the doorstep. Bobbi Jr whispered that he was ready.

The snitch started crying again, whispering that they didn't want to die. Dee didn't look at them. He looked at the door.
Because the engine outside wasn't just a threat.
It was a countdown.
And the family knew — Chapter Thirty-One wouldn't be quiet.

CHAPTER THIRTY-TWO — The Engine That Wouldn't Leave

The engine outside kept idling, low and steady, like a heartbeat in the dark. It didn't rev again. It didn't move. It didn't shift. It just sat there, humming through the walls, vibrating through the floorboards, pressing against the family's nerves like a weight they couldn't shake. Dee stood in the center of the living room, his body still, his eyes locked on the front door, his mind calculating every possibility. Corey hovered near the window, careful not to be seen, his breath shallow. Bev stood in the kitchen doorway, her hands trembling even as she tried to hide it.

Kayla sat at the dining table, her laptop open but untouched, her eyes sharp and unblinking. Aunt Jane whispered prayers under her breath, each one wrapping around the house like invisible armor. Bobbi Jr paced behind the couch, his fists clenched, his jaw tight, his spirit restless.

The snitch curled into the corner, shaking violently, whispering that the engine meant Red was here. That Red was watching. That Red was waiting. Dee didn't look at them. He didn't need to. The fear rolling off the snitch was loud enough to fill the room. Kayla finally spoke, her voice low but steady as she said the engine wasn't random. It wasn't a scare tactic. It was a signal. A presence. A placeholder. She said Red wasn't improvising — he was executing.

Corey whispered that the car wasn't moving because it didn't need to. Bev whispered that she felt like the house was shrinking. Aunt Jane whispered that darkness always lingered before it struck. Bobbi Jr whispered that he was tired of being hunted.

Dee stepped closer to the door, but he didn't open it. He didn't call out. He didn't show fear. He just listened. The engine hummed, steady and unbothered, like whoever sat inside wasn't in a rush. Like they were waiting for something. Or someone. The snitch lifted their head, tears streaking down their face, whispering that Red didn't trust them anymore. They said Red thought they were slipping. They said Red sent someone to "check on them" earlier.

They said Red wanted one thing — a moment of vulnerability. A crack. A slip. A mistake. Kayla leaned forward, her voice sharp as she said Red wasn't planning chaos — he was planning precision. Corey nodded,

whispering that the engine was part of the plan. Bev whispered that she didn't want to hear any more. Aunt Jane whispered that truth didn't care about comfort. Bobbi Jr whispered that they needed to act.

Then — the engine revved. Not loud. Not aggressive. Just enough to remind them it was still there. Dee didn't flinch. He didn't blink. He didn't move.

He said Red wasn't circling anymore. He wasn't mapping. He wasn't testing.

He was waiting. Kayla moved to the window, careful not to be seen, her voice low as she said the car hadn't moved an inch. Corey whispered that the block felt like it was holding its breath. Bev whispered that she felt like something was about to break. Aunt Jane whispered that the storm had reached the doorstep. Bobbi Jr whispered that he was ready.

The snitch started crying again, whispering that they didn't want to die. Dee didn't look at them. He looked at the door. Because the engine outside wasn't just a threat. It was a countdown. And the family knew —

CHAPTER THIRTY-THREE — The Bang That Split the Bloodline

The engine outside didn't just idle — it settled into the block like it belonged there, like it had been waiting for this moment since the first crack in the family formed back in Book One. Dee felt the shift before anyone else, the way the air tightened, the way the night grew still, the way the 44 seemed to lean in as if it knew history was about to change. Corey hovered near the window, careful not to be seen, his breath shallow and uneven. Bev stood in the kitchen doorway, whispering a prayer she hadn't said since the early days of the war.

Kayla closed her laptop with a slow, deliberate motion, her eyes sharp, her mind already calculating the angles. Aunt Jane whispered protection over the house, her voice steady even as the walls vibrated with tension. Bobbi Jr moved closer to Dee, his fists clenched, his jaw tight, his spirit ready for whatever storm stepped out of that car. And the snitch — broken, shaking, unraveling — curled into the corner, whispering that this was the moment Red had been building toward since the beginning.

Then came the knock — not on the door, but on the wall — three slow, measured taps that carried the weight of four books' worth of tension. Corey's breath caught, Bev gasped, Kayla froze, Aunt Jane whispered faster, and Bobbi Jr stepped forward, but Dee didn't move. The taps came again on the opposite side of the house, a cold reminder that Red wasn't knocking to be let in; he was knocking to announce that the war had reached its final phase. The snitch screamed as a whisper slid through the siding, a low, familiar voice saying **"Time's up."** Dee stepped toward the door, expression unreadable, body steady, listening as the house held its breath.

Then it happened — a single crack, sharp and explosive, close enough to shake the windows and split the night open. Bev screamed, Corey ducked, Kayla grabbed the table, Aunt Jane clutched her chest, Bobbi Jr lunged forward, and the snitch collapsed to the floor. Dee didn't move. The block went silent, the air frozen, until a car door slammed hard and fast, followed by the engine roaring back to life and tires screeching as the car tore down the street and disappeared into the darkness.

Only then did Dee turn around, and the truth hit the room like another gunshot — someone inside the house was bleeding. Not dead. Not gone. But hit. And it wasn't the snitch. Red hadn't aimed for the weakest link; he had aimed for the one person whose injury would fracture the entire bloodline, the one person whose fall would shake the 44 to its core, the one person whose pain would ignite the final war. As Dee dropped to his knees beside them, the family realized Red hadn't ended anything tonight.

He had opened the door to Book Five.
Book Four ends. The bloodline war begins.

CHAPTER ONE — After the Bang BOOK FIVE — OPENING CHAPTER TEASER

The house was still shaking from the gunshot when Dee pressed his hand against the wound, his breath steady even as the room spun with panic. Corey hovered near the window, whispering that the car was gone, that the street was empty, that Red had vanished into the night like smoke. Bev cried quietly in the kitchen doorway, her hands trembling as she tried to pray through the shock. Kayla moved fast, grabbing towels, applying pressure, her voice sharp and focused even as her eyes filled with fear. Aunt Jane whispered over the wounded body, her prayer steady, layered, powerful, wrapping the room in something stronger than panic. Bobbi Jr paced like a caged storm, fists clenched, jaw tight, whispering that Red had crossed a line that couldn't be uncrossed.

The snitch sat frozen in the corner, staring at the blood on the floor, whispering that this wasn't supposed to happen, that Red wasn't supposed to hit inside the house, that the plan wasn't supposed to go this far. Dee didn't look at them. He didn't have to. The betrayal was already written in the air, thick and sour, clinging to the walls like smoke.

The wounded person tried to speak, but Dee shook his head, telling them to save their strength. His voice was calm, but his eyes were fire — cold, focused, unshakeable. Kayla whispered that they needed to move them to the back room, away from the windows, away from the line of sight.

Corey nodded, already clearing the path. Bev whispered that she couldn't believe Red had done this. Aunt Jane whispered that she could — darkness always struck where the light was strongest. Bobbi Jr whispered that he wanted Red's head.

Dee lifted the wounded person carefully, his arms steady, his breath controlled, his mind already shifting into war mode. The house felt different now — heavier, darker, sharper. The 44 outside was silent, watching, listening, waiting. The block knew something had changed. Something irreversible. Something that would echo through every alley, every porch, every whispered conversation.

Kayla checked the window again, her voice low as she said Red wasn't done. She said the shot wasn't the attack — it was the announcement. Corey swallowed hard, whispering that the real move was coming. Bev whispered that she felt it too. Aunt Jane whispered that the enemy had declared war. Bobbi Jr whispered that they needed to strike first.

Dee laid the wounded person on the couch, his hands steady even as blood soaked through the towel. He looked around the room — at his family, at the snitch, at the walls that had protected them for years — and something inside him shifted. Something deep. Something final.

He said Red made one mistake.
He didn't finish the job.
The room froze.

Kayla looked up. Corey stopped breathing. Bev covered her mouth. Aunt Jane whispered a prayer of strength. Bobbi Jr stepped forward. The snitch shook harder.

Dee stood tall, his voice low and cold as he said the words **"We're not hiding anymore."**

The block outside stayed silent. The night held its breath. The war officially began.

ABOUT THE AUTHOR

Cece Vance is a creative visionary, retired celebrity publicist, entrepreneur, and author whose work blends heart, heritage, and hard-earned wisdom. Born with a storyteller's spirit and shaped by the powerful women in her family, Cece has spent her life building brands, nurturing talent, and creating spaces where culture, truth, and empowerment can thrive.

After more than a decade running her own PR company and launching the successful I Am You Natural Hair Care line, Cece expanded her creative reach into publishing — writing children's books, youth educational materials, adult learning tools, and now, emotionally charged urban fiction. Her stories are rooted in authenticity, family, and the unbreakable ties of the bloodline, drawing inspiration from her deep connection to Houston's creative and urban communities.

Cece's writing is a tribute to the people who shaped her — especially her beloved Aunt Jane, whose wisdom and love continue to guide every page. She also honors the memory of Bobbi Jr, whose legacy lives on through the emotional heartbeat of her work. A proud wife, mother, bonus mom, and grandmother, Cece writes with purpose, passion, and a commitment to representation. Whether she's crafting educational experiences for neurodiverse learners or building multi-book arcs set in the 44, Cece brings clarity, elegance, and cultural pride to every project.

Made in the USA
Coppell, TX
28 January 2026

70231856R10066